24 windows

ORSOLYA KISS-TOTH

First published in Great Britain in 2023
This edition published in 2023.

Cover design by Lena Yang

A catalogue record for this book is available from the British Library.

Paperback ISBN 978-1-7394843-0-9
eBook ISBN 978-1-7394843-1-6

Here's to learning how to live in the moment whilst following a dream

Prologue

It was only words and words could never physically harm you. Or could they? The question flashed through Annabel Tate's mind.

She was inclined to disagree as she mentally scanned the scabbed-over wounds of her past. They weren't visible to the naked eye, but to her they felt as real and raw as the graze on her arm when she came off her bike at age seven.

Or the sting of hearing the dismissive tone, the underwhelmed reaction that followed a school competition prize, as if she expected her to do better. By the time she got to her graduation and landed her first job she wasn't sure if she could be outwardly excited about her achievements. If that was allowed or appropriate, or if she was just exaggerating something trivial.

She thought she'd grown used to failure being her default, but somehow it still hurt. Despite the knockbacks, she still thought she could live up to her mother's expectations, but she was quickly reminded that the bar was set high.

'Maybe it was time to rethink this career path of yours. Settle down, have your own family.' Her mother's remarks rang in her ear and somehow, she couldn't dismiss them anymore.

A familiar discomfort returned again, and with every word it spread fast across all her senses. Her heart thumped furiously, her jaw tightened, and her cheeks flushed as she dug her fingernails firmly into her palm; her knuckles turning even whiter than usual.

Will she swallow the hurt again and let it keep brewing under the surface or face the unknown? What was it going to be? The choice was hers to make alone.

Chapter 1

Annabel Tate stood on platform five staring in the direction of the tracks as if waiting for a train. She had done this many times before on the way home from work, but today was different. Today, there was no one else around. The trains came and went one after the other, but Annabel didn't move. People had rushed past her and slowly the station drained of commuters. The few that arrived were huddled under the roof, sheltering from the pounding November rain. But not Annabel. She had been standing there motionless for over an hour, the rain pouring down her face, masking the streaks of tears. She was cold and numb, but none of that mattered.

In her head she went over what had happened again and again. Trying to remember every word to find where it all went wrong. She had been so sure that this time it was her turn; she didn't allow an inch of doubt. There was no other way. She had to be right. She wanted to rewind the clock. How far back she wasn't sure. A week, a month or maybe more.

Her stomach fizzed as she thought of Jonathan sitting across the table from her just a few hours before. The initial compliments felt so faint Annabel even questioned their existence.

'I'm really sorry to tell you, but we've decided to give the position to Sandra. It was such a close call and if we had two roles to fill, we'd have been able to give you the opportunity as well.'

But she knew these were empty words. Roles like these were rare, and if they came up, internal applicants weren't usually considered.

Exactly two months ago, it all seemed possible when an email landed in her inbox, with the subject line *Editorial Opening*. Her reserved demeanour didn't often allow for huge outward displays of emotion, but the excitement was almost too much to keep inside.

She had worked as an editorial assistant for Herold & Hains for over seven years and becoming an editor was all she'd ever wanted to do. At first she was quiet, wanting to learn as much as she could, soaking up every bit of knowledge around her. And despite her insecurities, she took every opportunity she could to show her bosses that she was made for this role and that she wanted it more than anything. She often worked long hours and weekends to prove she was committed, taking on extra projects to show them she was ready to move up the ranks.

In the early stages, despite her valid contributions she often felt inadequate, an imposter. Nevertheless, she ploughed on with determination. But something had to give, and it was her relationships and personal life that paid the price for hanging onto a dream. She knew that there was only a fine line separating grit and determination from single-minded madness. And to reassure herself, she chose to identify with the former.

She knew this editorial opportunity would make all the sacrifice worth it; it would prove to herself and everyone that had doubted her that she had what it took to succeed.

The excitement she felt when she received that email was long gone.

She had battled with her demons throughout the process, but she almost allowed herself to be pleased when she made it to the final round with only her and Sandra in the running.

With the finish line in sight, she worked late into the night to get her pitch perfect. The panic that she felt when she thought she'd lost the file as she fell asleep over her computer still made her shiver. If it wasn't for her neighbour's, James's help in locating the missing presentation, the whole thing could have ended there, with nothing to present at that final stage.

But what difference would it have made?

This wasn't the first time she'd faced rejection, but this latest defeat felt even worse than the ones before.

Jonathan's rejection still rang in her ears.

How could they give it to Sandra? Of all people, why her?

Her limbs felt numb, her chest tight and her jaws tingling. She'd wished she could vanish without having to hear the reasons for her inadequacy, but she wanted to know where she'd gone wrong.

'Is there anything that I could improve on in the future?' she asked quietly, her voice shaking slightly.

'Your ideas were original and sound. Please don't think there was anything wrong with them,' said Jonathan. 'Sandra just pitched something different from what we'd ever done before. It was a bold suggestion that showed great insight.'

A bold suggestion. The words reverberated in Annabel's mind. She was vexed with herself for not going with her initial idea. For choosing a safer path. Then an earlier conversation flashed through her mind. Sandra sounded like she was going to play it safe and go with a more popular option. If it wasn't for that exchange of words, her confidence in her original plan may have never wavered. She would have never thought of completely scrapping her pitch and coming up with a new one.

'Sounds intriguing,' said Annabel, trying to regain her composure.

'It is. We were wondering if you'd be interested in assisting Sandra on this project?' asked Thomas. As the Marketing Director he was part of the interview panel and he often got involved in the projects Annabel worked on. He had been silent up to this point, sitting on Jonathan's right.

'So, I'd work under Sandra?' asked Annabel, trying not to sound irritated. She could feel her cheeks flush with anger.

'No, you'd still report to me, but you'd work with her on this project. You don't have to answer right now, but I think you could really bring some great contributions. Just have a think about it before you decide,' said Jonathan.

Sensing that their discussion was drawing to an end, she quietly said, 'I will,' as she readied herself to leave. The tension in her jaw had slackened somewhat, but her indignation grew as she closed the door behind her.

Why didn't I stick with the Shaw manuscript? It might have been risky, but I could feel that it had legs. Maybe my mother was right. I should have stayed in Masham and managed the bookshop after all. And why did Sandra change her mind? But none of this would have been an issue if Annabel had trusted her instincts. A memoir style novel with Avery Poole, a fictional British secret agent in the centre of the story. Unlike other spy novels, this story focused on the inner workings of its protagonist. It had seemed that Sandra had no interest in the concept.

Annabel felt sick. Her initial panic and irritation had turned into something firmer, something unshakeable. That maybe this was it. Maybe she'd never be good enough to make the grade as an editor and she would be destined to follow other people's ideas and never to make her own mark. The emotions sat heavy in her throat like a dam ready to burst again letting through another wave of tears.

It was only the deep rumble of the sky that shook her out of her trance. Her skin prickled from the cold as the wet layers clung to it. She looked at the clock overhead. It had just gone seven. She shivered at the realisation that she'd been standing there for over an hour, unaware of her surroundings.

The lights of the approaching train cut through the drizzle, and she stepped back, watching the carriage come to a halt and people dribble out of the doors. Still numb, she checked the overhead sign for the destination before stepping inside and taking a seat.

Sitting there wiping water off herself, she turned to look at her reflection in the window. The remnants of her mascara were still visible on her face. She took out a compact mirror to inspect the damage. Her cheeks were flushed, and her eyes burned red. She felt her eyes filling up with tears again as the train made its way out of the station. She shut the compact and swallowed a sob before the cycle could begin again. She was grateful to be sitting alone, away from the concern of others. She couldn't wait to get home.

She took her phone out and the screen flashed up, alerting her to five missed calls, all from David. She hovered over the icon next to his name and hesitated for a second. She needed a sympathetic ear, someone to tell her that things were going to be okay. But would he understand? She couldn't be sure. She tapped on the icon, listening to the rings before David's voice greeted her.

'Finally! I was worried about you. You haven't answered any of my calls. Is everything okay?'

'Yeah, sorry. My phone was still on silent.'

'How did it go, then? Did you get the job?' His voice was full of anticipation.

'I...,' Annabel's voice cracked as she replied. 'They gave it to Sandra.'

'That sucks.' He sighed. 'So that's it, then. No more late nights or working weekends.'

Annabel didn't respond for a second. She knew what David wanted. She'd promised him that once this job came through, she'd have a less hectic work schedule and more time for him. But instead, she was exactly where she was before. Her dream still in sight, but just out of reach. Could she call it a day and accept defeat?

'I agreed to help Jonathan on a project for next week. I might need to do a few things this weekend,' she replied finally.

'This weekend? I thought we'd agreed, Annabel. It's Aunt Lou's 60th birthday party and I told everyone you're coming along, finally.'

'I'm sorry. Jonathan asked and I couldn't say no. If I decline now, they might not consider me next time there's an opportunity.'

'Next time? You've been trying for years, Annabel. Why can't you just accept that this is it? You have a good job, the pay is okay and once you work normal hours we can finally have a life outside of Herold & Hains.'

'But what if that's not good enough for me?' Asked Annabel her voice shaking as she dug her fingernails into her palm. 'Is it so bad to have a dream and to work for making it a reality?'

'It is when you have no life beyond it,' said David with resignation.

There was a moment of silence before he spoke again.

'I can't do this anymore, Annabel. I'm just tired of trying to be your priority. Or at least to be one of them.'

'But you are.'

'No. Your career is.'

'David, please,' pleaded Annabel swallowing a sob as a lump gathered in her throat. Her heart was racing as she felt the weight of what was coming, desperate to stop it. 'This is the last time, I promise.'

'You know it's not. Goodbye, Annabel.'

The line went silent, and Annabel collapsed on the table in front of her, the tears she'd held back throughout the phone call pouring onto the back of her hands. She felt broken and alone. For a moment she thought of ringing David back, *but what would be the point?* The voice in her head told her that maybe he was right.

The rain had stopped by the time she got off the train, and she had managed to regain some of her composure. The cold wind kept her anchored in reality as she walked along the high street from the station. Exhausted, she fumbled in her coat pocket for her keys as she got to her flat. She was startled when James stuck his head around his door.

'Are we still on for dinner tonight?' he asked eagerly.

She had no time to hide her confusion. It took her a few seconds before she remembered that she promised to cook him dinner in return for last night's rescue mission. Annabel's reaction was so automatic. She had no time to hide her confusion.

'You forgot,' he exclaimed.

'I'm so sorry. I didn't have the best of days.'

'Oh, sorry. We can rain check if you're not feeling up to it.'

Entertaining someone was the last thing Annabel felt like doing, but she hated to let James down, especially after everything he'd done the night before. She had to admit that being alone and feeling sorry for herself wasn't exactly a great alternative either.

'No, I'm all right. Just give me twenty minutes and I'll rustle something up.'

'How about I order some food and you can tell me what happened that made you forget my dinner?' said James with a smile.

Annabel hesitated for a moment. 'Sounds good,' she said eventually.

'I'm stuffed,' said James as he leant back on his chair.

'The food was delicious, but you should have let me pay for it at least,' said Annabel.

'Don't worry about it. You can cook next time. You've been awfully quiet tonight. I hope I didn't impose on you.'

'You didn't. It's just... Things didn't turn out as I hoped today.'

'I guessed that much. What happened? I mean only if you want to talk about it. Otherwise just tell me to mind my own business.'

Annabel hesitated for a second before she answered.

'I didn't get the job and David broke up with me,' she said, her voice wobbling.

'That sucks,' said James. His body stiffened slightly as his eyes darted to Annabel, taking a moment before he continued. 'David's a fool. I know it's not my place, but you're probably better off without him if he can't see how great you are,' he said, placing his hand on Annabel's.

'Thanks. That makes me feel slightly less crappy about the whole thing,' said Annabel, her lips turning to a smile momentarily. 'But I think he had a point,' she added with resignation.

'We'll agree to disagree,' replied James in a slightly cheerier tone.

'I know you're being nice, but maybe I'm not made for this relationship stuff. I just can't seem to find a balance.'

'I get that you're upset but give it a few weeks and you might have a different outlook.'

'I don't know. I think it's best I burry my head in work and quit dating for a while,' said Annabel with defiance, pushing her plate to one side.

Sensing that Annabel wasn't ready to consider other options, James steered the conversation onto another topic. 'Speaking of work, what happened with the interview?' Feeling a pause, he added quickly. 'You don't have to talk about it if you'd rather not.'

'No, it's fine. And to be honest, I'm still not quite sure what happened. Everything was going so well. They seemed to like the presentation and I thought I'd got it in the bag. But then, they chose this other person. Sandra. It's not that she doesn't deserve it. Clearly, she must have done a better job than me. It's just that she's only been with the company for like a year and she's already ahead of me. I've been waiting for this opportunity for so long. I've put everything into it. Not just this presentation, but everything over the last seven years.'

'That must be hard. So, what are you going to do now?'

'I don't know. I still have my job at least, and they asked me to consider working with Sandra on this new project. I was livid when they mentioned it at first. The thought of working under her... But it might be a good opportunity. I just don't know what to do anymore.'

'Yeah, that doesn't sound good. I'm certainly no expert on publishing or book editing, but can I give you, my advice?'

'Sure,' replied Annabel, a little hesitant.

'I've been in a place before where I kept pursuing a career just because I felt I'd put so much into it, and I couldn't just give it up. But there came a time when I had no other option but to walk away from it. I wasn't sleeping, my relationship broke down and eventually my mental health took a bad turn. Sometimes you've got to know when to stop trying. It doesn't sound like you've had much luck at this place. Maybe it's time to consider trying somewhere else.'

Leaving publishing had crossed Annabel's mind before, but this wasn't the advice she was expecting. She'd wanted reassurance that she was probably close to her breakthrough and that she shouldn't give up. Instead, she was told to stop trying.

'I wish it was that easy. I can't just walk away from it all. I've worked far too hard for far too long to start all over again.'

'I can imagine how you feel and I'm not saying it's an easy path either, but in the long run it might be better for you. I found it hard to make the change, but looking back on it now, it was totally the right thing to do.'

'Was it your dream job, the one you gave up?' asked Annabel. James always seemed so content. She'd never considered that he wasn't living the life he always wanted.

'Kind of. When I got what I thought I wanted, I realised it didn't make me happy. In fact, I was stressed out a lot of the time.'

'But at least you got to live out that dream and decide that it wasn't for you. I haven't even got to that point yet.'

'But what's the point of pursuing it if it's making you feel miserable? Aren't you supposed to love what you do every day?' His question hung in the air between them, Annabel not ready to answer. 'Like I said before, this is only my take on it, and you can ignore me if you like, but if I was you, I'd be looking for something else or at least somewhere else.'

Annabel stared at the empty plate in front of her.

'Anyway, I should get going,' said James.

'So, you're not going to tell me about this forgotten dream of yours?' asked Annabel.

'The dream wasn't forgotten, it just changed. But maybe another time. You must be tired.'

Annabel didn't protest; she was feeling mentally and emotionally drained.

'Just knock on my door if you need anything,' he said, before he left.

Annabel retrieved a tub of salted caramel ice cream from the freezer as her thoughts turned to his advice. James was always calm and annoyingly often right. And she didn't like his advice one bit. Despite feeling defeated and not quite knowing what to do next, she didn't think that giving up was the right thing to do, but more importantly, she wasn't sure if she was ready to let go.

A couple of days passed, and Annabel was no closer to arriving at a decision about her future direction. Sensing it was time to leave her flat, she made plans for the evening and was just about to leave when the phone rang.

'How are you, darling?'

Somehow her mother could always sense the most inconvenient times to call.

'Mum, what a nice surprise. It's not the best time though. I'm about to leave. I'm meeting Lucy for dinner.'

'Oh! I thought you might be going out with David, but dinner with Lucy sounds nice too.'

Crap! thought Annabel. She felt miserable enough about the past week's events, and she completely forgot that she would have to tell her mother about the breakup at some point. Another round of feeling like a total failure that she couldn't handle just yet.

'We've got to be quick, Mum. I need to get going in a minute.'

'Don't worry, I won't keep you for long. Just wanted to discuss with you about having your dress fitted for Abi's wedding.'

'Now? The wedding is still ages away.'

'It's only a few months and you know what your sister is like. She likes to get everything sorted well in advance.'

'Yes, I know. Why didn't she ring me, anyway?'

'She's busy with organising everything and work has been hectic at the practice; so, I offered to help out.'

Of course, you did. 'That's nice of you. When is she thinking?'

'She wants it sorted before Christmas. Just so she has one less thing to worry about.'

Annabel reached for the glass of water on the table and took a sip before she replied. 'I'll see if I can get away, but I can't promise anything.'

'It'd be good if you could but let me know either way. How are you otherwise?'

'I'm okay. Work's busy, as usual.'

'Have you heard back about your promotion yet?'

Annabel hesitated, picking bits of fluff off her blanket on the sofa. She knew she would have to tell her mother at some point, but she had hoped it wouldn't be until she'd got over the initial phase of self-pity and doubt. She couldn't lie and her mother's question had backed her into a corner, leaving her no choice but to confess.

'I didn't get it.'

'Really? That's such a shame. You could have been running the book shop here by now, you know.'

Annabel gripped the edge of her blanket, holding her breath, her knuckles turning whiter and whiter.

'Mum, I really don't want to get into this conversation again. We've been through this before,' she said finally.

'I know, but it's been such a long time and if they haven't promoted you so far what are the chances of them offering you the position now?'

Her mother's words hit a nerve. It didn't matter whether she was right or not, Annabel just wished her mother could be on her side for once. All she wanted was her sympathy, her encouragement that everything would work out in the end. But she should have known she couldn't count on her for that.

'I need to go, Mum. I'm running late already. I'll let you know about the dress fitting.'

'All right. Say hi to Lucy for me.'

By the time she'd hung up the phone it was twenty to seven and she had a fifteen-minute train ride to get to the city and a walk from the station to Dim Sum Bay. As she rushed out the door she nearly ran into an elderly gentleman in the corridor.

'These young people are always in a rush,' he mumbled.

'I'm so sorry,' said Annabel quickly before picking the pace back up to catch her train.

Lucy was sat by the bar when Annabel arrived.

'I'm sorry I'm late. I hope you haven't been waiting too long,' apologised Annabel as she reached her friend.

'I've only had one of these so far,' said Lucy pointing at the empty glass in front of her. 'You might want to try one. It's not as good as the real thing but it's close enough.'

'What was it?'

'A Mockito, I think. Are you all right? You look a bit flustered.'

Over dinner Annabel told Lucy all about the ordeals of the week: her meltdown when she thought she had lost her submission piece, how James helped her retrieve it, and- how she still missed out on the editorial job. She took a drink of water, her throat raw from talking. 'And then, when I thought things couldn't get any worse, David decided to end things between us,' she said as she exhaled, her shoulders dropping slightly.

'Why didn't you call me?' asked Lucy, her eyes soft.

'For you to listen to me sob for an hour? I felt exhausted, and I didn't want to burden you with all this on an evening. I needed to get my head straight first.'

'David's a numpty,' said Lucy, placing her hand on Annabel's.

'I know you're being nice, but I think he had a point. My life is a mess.'

'That's a bit of an exaggeration,' said Lucy. 'But life is messy. I'll tell you about something that happened to me the other day. I was trying to get the girls into the car ready for nursery and school on Thursday before heading to my doctor's appointment when Ivy threw up on me. I got changed and was finally ready to go when Nelly decided she needed the toilet. By the time I pulled up outside the nursery Ivy was completely fine. I still think it was her wolfing down her breakfast too quickly. Anyway, I don't know how, but by some miracle I made it to the doctor's on time. I was so pleased with myself and then when I sat in the waiting room, I realised that my shoes didn't match. Dr Lane called my name and I just burst into tears pointing at my shoes. Thankfully she was so understanding. She's seen enough pregnant people before having a meltdown. I blame the hormones,' Lucy laughed.

'Oh Lucy, I'm so sorry. You've got your own stuff to deal with. You don't need to hear about my misery too.'

'Oh, please. What is a best friend for? Plus talking about anything other than Peppa Pig at the moment sounds like a real treat to be honest. I'm up half the night anyway, either needing a pee or a snack so it's not like I'm fast asleep. And it's not like you've never listened to my problems.'

'Still.'

'So, what are you going to do now?'

'I don't know. They've offered me to work under Sandra on this project. She's hardly been there for a year, and they thought she'd do a better job than me and now they want me to work with her.

'That sucks.'

'It does.'

'So did you tell them where to stick it?'

Annabel fiddled with the chopsticks before she answered. 'No. I told them I'd think about it,' she said lifting her eyes to meet Lucy's. 'Don't look at me like that. It could still be a great opportunity.'

'Hmmm,' replied Lucy.

'And just to really rub salt in the wound, my mother rang just as I was leaving home today giving me her usual unsolicited advice. She says hi by the way.'

'Just ignore her, you know what she's like.'

'It's not that easy, Lucy. I don't know why she likes telling me how I've failed at life and how I should pack in this editorial malarkey. She finds great satisfaction in pointing out that I was wrong, and she was right. She's convinced that I should've accepted the job to manage the bookshop back home when I had the chance. I know she means well, but it's as if she doesn't know me at all. Or if she does, she doesn't seem to care much about what I want to do with my life. I bet when she finds out she'll tell me that David was right for ending things.'

'You haven't told her?'

'I just couldn't bring myself to do it. I know she's not doing it on purpose, or at least I hope she doesn't intentionally make me feel such a failure, but she really has a knack for it.'

Lucy looked thoughtful, tapping her fingers on the outside of her glass. 'This is probably the last thing you want to hear, but I'm going to be frank with you, my dear,' started Lucy. 'I'm not saying your mother or David is right or that you can't follow your dreams, but I can't remember the last time I saw you happy. This job has consumed your life for so long. As much as that might be what you want, what's the point if it isn't making you happy? When was the last time you did something for you?' she asked.

Annabel was just about to reply, but Lucy held out a hand, cutting her off. 'And that wasn't for work?'

Annabel sighed. 'That's kind of what James said last night. I know you're both right in a way, but this is what I've been working for all these years. The late nights, the working weekends, the cancelled dates with David, the missed holidays. It was all for nothing if I quit now.' Annabel paused for a moment before she carried on. 'Without this, I'm not so sure I know who I am anymore.' Annabel's eyes clouded over slightly as her words reverberated in her mind.

'Hey. Of course, you are. This job doesn't define you,' said Lucy gently. 'And I'm not saying you should quit. But maybe you could take some time out for yourself. And I've got just the idea. Why don't you join me at my next book club event? It's a week on Thursday at six thirty. We usually pick a book and talk about that but this time we'll be discussing what we've read this month. I always get great ideas for my reading list. I know it'd be right up your street.' she continued. 'It's a great place to meet new people and it could be something nice you could do for yourself for a change'.

Annabel felt too drained to come up with an excuse and she thought she might actually enjoy a distraction. And, as always, Lucy was right: this was her kind of thing. So, after some thought, she agreed to go along.

Later that night Annabel stared into the darkness as she lay on her bed, Lucy's words still ringing in her ears.

Am I happy?

She'd never really paused or dared to ask herself the question and now that it was staring her in the face, she wanted to flee rather than think about the answer. For many years she'd crafted this image of what it meant to be happy and when she could finally put it into words, she'd spent a lot of time convincing others of that too. But what if this wasn't it? She'd made a conscious decision to focus on her career when she thought that sacrificing her social life, love life and putting everything else on hold would only be temporary. She felt that her mother wanted her to bow down to the shackles of convention. To follow the well-walked path of marriage and children in favour of fulfilling her professional dream. But Annabel felt these things wouldn't make her happy in the end. Not without the professional accomplishments, anyway.

It's not that she never thought about marriage or having children, but David didn't seem to be in a rush either and she had thought she could have all that when she was ready. When she was fulfilled in her career. *But what if that day never came? What if her mother and David were both right? What if all the sacrifice was for nothing in the end?*

She felt her throat tighten. The idea scared her, but she knew she couldn't allow herself to be wrapped up in any more self-doubt. *Got to stop thinking like that. Something will come up soon enough,* she thought. Despite trying to reassure herself, James's words came to the front of her mind as she closed her eyes. A sense of unease remained, but not at the thought of failure, rather at the thought of success.

***

During the days that followed Annabel tried to stay busy at work and refocus her mind to reassure herself that things would be back on track soon enough. She agreed to work with Sandra on the new project and the date for the kick-off meeting was set. It was also officially announced that Sandra had been promoted to the editorial position and she'd replied to a number of 'I'm sorry you didn't get the job' emails from her colleagues.

She headed to the café on the third floor. Just after half past ten, timing it so the morning regulars were gone and it was too early for lunch. She was busy trying to decide between a blueberry muffin and a cheese croissant when someone came up next to her.

'Oh, those muffins look so delicious,' exclaimed Sandra. 'If it wasn't for the twenty or so syns I'd have them every day.'

Startled, Annabel tried to regain her composure. Sandra always seemed to be overly excited about the most mundane of things.

'Syns?' she asked, puzzled.

This was the first time the two of them had been alone together since Sandra's promotion and despite accepting to work on the new project with her, Sandra was the last person Annabel wanted to chat with.

Annabel fumbled in her purse for a few moments before she broke the silence between them. 'Congratulations on the role,' she said finally.

'Thank you. I'm sorry you missed out on it. But hey, you still get to work on the project so it's not that different really, is it?' Sandra smiled. Without waiting for a reply, Sandra turned to the barista, pushing in front of Annabel.

'A skinny soy latte please with extra cinnamon on the top to take away.'

'I hope you don't mind,' she said, turning to Annabel with an overly sweet smile. 'I've got to dash. We're having a pre-project meeting before the official kick-off.'

'Sure, you go ahead,' said Annabel.

'I'll go for the muffin and a regular latte please,' said Annabel when Sandra left. 'I think I deserve a few syns. Whatever they are.'

It was the day of the book club and Annabel found herself getting excited about it. She was more than halfway through a book, and she was really getting into it. She thought it would be a great one to recommend to the group. Still feeling somewhat wronged, she decided to leave work on time.

As she stepped out onto the street, she felt the sharp shock of cold against her warm skin. It was a clear November night and her breath hung in the still air as she exhaled. She wrapped her scarf a little tighter and pulled her mittens on as she started to walk along the pavement. In the distance, a glimmer of colourful lights attracted her attention. The Christmas decorations had gone up a few weeks earlier, but she had been too wrapped up in her thoughts lately to notice. The bookshop was only four stops away and she still had plenty of time, so she decided to take a closer look at the festive decorations and walk instead.

The bustling high street was busy with shoppers. Some rushing about, some just taking in the sights, admiring the lifelike winter window displays. Waves of fairy lights sparkled overhead in the arcades like swarms of fireflies. But the pinnacle of the extravaganza was the large Christmas tree in the main square showered with a rainbow of shimmering lights. The sight was truly spectacular. She wasn't sure why the sight of colourful lights felt so mesmerising, but she quickly found herself getting into the festive spirit. The tree was adorned with large baubles, and a young woman in an elf costume was giving out small cards with envelopes.

'Make a wish and hang it on the tree,' she said, handing one to Annabel.

'I'm all right, thank you,' she replied.

'It's only a wish. I'm sure you have one,' she smiled.

Reluctantly, Annabel took the card and rummaged around in her bag looking for a pen. After a few seconds of fruitless searching, she gave up and tucked the card and the envelope into her coat pocket.

She got to the shop about fifteen minutes early and others were already there, busy helping with the set-up. Lucy was about to move a couple of chairs around when a woman in her fifties said to her in an overprotective manner. 'Just leave the heavy lifting to me.'

Lucy spotted Annabel and beamed. 'Hey,' she said. 'So glad you came!'

'I'd have never heard the end of it if I didn't show up,' she replied, hugging her friend. 'Joke aside, I've been looking forward to it.'

Lucy turned to her friend. 'This is Annabel. My friend I told you about last time,' she said.

'So lovely to meet you, Annabel. I'm Julie. I run this bookshop and put the events on once a month,' the woman said, greeting Annabel. 'You're a book editor, aren't you? How exciting!'

'Editorial assistant,' Annabel added quickly, feeling her cheeks flush.

'It's all the same to me.' She smiled. 'It's great to have you with us tonight.'

'Really nice to meet you too. I've heard great things about the club,' replied Annabel.

Lucy introduced her friend to the others in the group. Joy, a book club veteran and lover of gothic fiction; Harlow, a keen fantasy reader; Owen, who seemed to be a walking-talking book of historical facts; and Helen, who reminded Annabel of a fairy godmother. They were all keen to find out what it was like to work in publishing and probed her to see if she could reveal anything about long-awaited sequels.

Eventually, everyone took their seats and they were just about to start when the shop door jingled, and a man with rosy cheeks walked in.

'Sorry I'm late,' he mumbled as he made his way to the only empty chair, opposite Annabel.

'Not to worry Alex, you didn't miss anything. We were just about to make a start,' said Julie.

He took his seat and Annabel smiled at him as their eyes met.

Julie started off the discussion with her recommendation of Namina Forna's latest book.

'It's a great one. I think you'd like this one Harlow,' said Julie.

In turn, Harlow was keen to share her experiences about the new Naomi Novik book.

'It was so captivating,' said Harlow.

Lucy's pick of the month was Jessie Burton's *The Confession.* Owen talked about his views on Umberto Eco's *The Name of the Rose* and Helen got everyone in the festive spirit by telling them about her latest read of Christmas short stories.

'What about you, Annabel?' asked Julie.

For the last month most of her reading centred around the work she reviewed for her presentation. With Shaw's manuscript still firmly in the back of her mind she wished she could share the story of the British spy struggling to reconcile his personal and professional personas with the rest of the group. But knowing they wouldn't be able to read the story themselves, or at least not for a while, she decided against it. 'I've read a few things recently, but I'm re-reading Henrik Ibsen's *A Doll's House* at the moment. I know it was designed for stage, but the themes at the heart of the story are so relevant today. Ibsen might not have intended it to be a feminist story, but it sure placed the role of women in relationships under scrutiny. It's interesting to think how far society has come from those times in the 1870s and perhaps asks whether we've come far enough.'

'A great story, for sure,' replied Alex. 'I'm actually playing Torvald at the moment at the Playhouse.'

'Oh, really?' replied Annabel, sounding a little more eager than she wanted to.

'How exciting,' joined in Julie.

Alex gathered an audience and soon the conversation was steered towards his acting career, but he didn't seem to mind.

After about fifteen minutes of discussion, Julie tried to bring the conversation back to books. 'We got a bit off topic there didn't we? Have you read anything exciting recently, Alex?' she asked.

'A couple of things actually, but one that really stuck with me was a book by Toshikazu Kawaguchi. *Before the Coffee Gets Cold.* Not sure if any of you've read it. There's time travel involved, but it's not so much about do overs in a sense that the characters can't say or do anything that would change their present when back in their past. It made me think of some questions I'd have asked if I had the chance to meet someone for one last time.'

Annabel fixed her eyes on Alex, and she only moved when his gaze met hers.

'Wow, we had so many great suggestions this evening. Can't remember the last time we had such a good round. Shall we have a vote on what you'd all like to read for next time?' asked Julie.

Following Julie's lead, they voted, and as predicted Alex's recommendation won out over the others. Helen wasn't sure about the choice but everyone else seemed keen to read Kawaguchi's book, so they agreed to discuss it next month.

'So, did you have a good time?' Lucy asked Annabel as they got ready to leave. 'You seemed to enjoy yourself.'

'I did, I'm not going to lie. And not just because of what you might think,' replied Annabel with a grin.

'I have no idea what you're referring to,' said Lucy, glancing over in Alex's direction.

'Thanks for nagging me to come along.'

'Nagging? I simply made a suggestion. Anyway, I knew you'd love it! I was a bit worried you might not come after the other day at the restaurant. I didn't mean to upset you. I just want you to be happy.'

'I know that. And you didn't upset me, so don't worry about it. We're all good.'

'I'm glad. So, you're going to come again next time?'

'Might do. I need to check my calendar first.' Noticing Lucy's expression, she quickly added. 'I'm only joking. Your face just can't hide any emotion.' Laughed Annabel.

Annabel felt content. It was one of the better days she'd had in weeks. She wished her life could be more fun an uncomplicated more often. 'Do you have a pen?' she asked Lucy, taking the Christmas wish card and envelope she was given earlier out of her pocket.

'Probably, let me have a look.'

Annabel scribbled something on the piece of paper and slid it into the envelope.

'Do you want a hand with that?' she asked, pointing at a gift bag next to Lucy.

'No, it's all right. I've only parked around the corner.'

'What's in it? Is it my Christmas present?' asked Annabel.

'You're very nosy. But no, it's not. It's something for Nelly. She's been writing letters to Santa asking for a doll house for weeks now.'

'How cute. Me and Abi used to have one. Loved playing with it.'

'Maybe you can ask Santa for one too.' Lucy smiled.

Chapter 2

December arrived with a spell of frost and fog. If it wasn't for the twinkling lights and decorations everywhere it would have been a miserable sight. It was the 1st of December and Annabel was enjoying her morning cup of coffee when the doorbell rang.

Who could this be? She picked up the intercom receiver. 'Hello?'

'I've got a delivery for Annabel Tate,' said the voice on the other end.

She let the man in and before she could guess who the delivery might be from, there was a knock on the door.

She wasn't sure what she was expecting, but the size of the parcel in front of her door sure took her by surprise.

'Can I have a signature, please?' asked the man.

'Sure. Who is it from?'

'Sorry, there are no details on here. There might be something inside the box though.'

Annabel thanked the man and closed the door, hauling the parcel into the living room with Marley following behind, meowing and nose twitching in curiosity. He seemed rather interested in the contents of the box as Annabel placed it on the table. She checked the label, and it was definitely addressed to her. With growing excitement, she started to look for a pair of scissors in the kitchen drawers.

'Why can't you ever find anything when you need it?' she muttered, slightly annoyed as she rummaged through the drawers, making a mental note to sort through them later. Faded receipts, piles of elastic bands, a couple of pens with no caps. But not a pair of scissors in sight.

After a few minutes of fruitless searching, she had finally found the scissors. Excited like a child at Christmas, she was eager to see what was inside, opening the cardboard box and shoving the packaging onto the floor, to Marley's delight.

Finally, she unveiled a red wooden box bearing the painted picture of a nutcracker on both sides. On one side, the nutcracker was dressed in a white and silver uniform, on the other, in green and gold. The paint was dry, but you could still smell the lacquer finish. She looked for a note amongst the wrapping on the floor, but there was nothing to give away the sender's identity.

The box felt heavy and robust, but the decoration gave it a delicate feel at the same time. Annabel was in awe of the craftsmanship, and carefully placed it on her dining table, admiring the detail and the finish. On one of the narrower sides of the box, brass hinges connected the two wooden panels. On the other, a brass clasp locked the two pieces together. As she fiddled with the clasp to open the box, a yellow envelope slid out onto the table. Her name was written across it in elegant, slanted letters, but she didn't recognise the handwriting. With some hesitation, she opened the envelope and pulled out a folded piece of paper. Intrigued, she began to read.

Dear Annabel,

I know that things haven't been going to plan for you lately and that there have been a few more snags along the way than one would like. I know you have been working hard for what you want, and that is admirable, but I can't help but feel that you've lost yourself a little along the way.

Christmas can be a beautiful time of year when most people take stock and re-evaluate what really matters in their lives. During the weeks of Advent, we tend to decorate our homes, catch up with friends and get ready for the festivities ahead. But more than that, we prepare our souls for something better to come and believe that happiness is just around the corner. We forgive and look ahead with great expectations, allowing ourselves to believe in the possibilities that would seem a bit far-fetched at other times of the year.
So, I ask you to keep an open mind when you open this gift and I hope that you'll embrace the challenge.

St. N.
P.S. Please don't be a Grinch!

Annabel wasn't quite sure what to make of the letter. *St. N.? Is this a joke?* The box stood in front of her like an open book. The images on the inside were even more intricate than on the outside. Adorned with motifs of the festive season, it was truly a piece of art. Inside it was left mostly unpainted, revealing the natural grain of the wood.

She ran her fingers across the smooth surface, inspecting the twelve windows on each side of the box, marked with twenty-four red numbers.

After some searching, she found the window marked with an elegant number one. Her natural curiosity seemed to have overwritten any initial apprehension she had. Excited, she reached to open the tiny door decorated with an innocent-looking gingerbread man.

When the window opened, a small scroll of paper tumbled out. Marley was quick to seize the opportunity and pounced on it.

'Get off it, Marley,' scolded Annabel as she shooed him away. Locating the piece of paper under the table, she gingerly unrolled it. Staring at it for quite some time, she re-read the text again and again, hoping to find a different meaning perhaps.

'What is this, a joke?' she exclaimed finally. She paced up and down the room searching her mind who could have sent her the box and more importantly, why?

Could David have something to do with this?

She dismissed the idea quickly. David didn't have much of an eye for anything artistic. He was the kind of guy who thought it was adventurous to choose a stripey tie instead of a plain one. *No, it can't be him.*

She picked up the letter again and ran her eyes over the lines once more. It didn't sound like her mother at all, but the box looked elegant, and she couldn't dismiss the thought that her mother could send something like this just to get Annabel to do what she wanted. The thought took a firmer root in Annabel's mind, conjuring up a million possibilities about what her mother might want to achieve. Maybe she had a plan to get Annabel back to Masham to run the bookshop.

She couldn't be sure it was her, but she had to find out somehow. She couldn't just call and ask her straight up. She would deny it. She had to find some proof somehow.

The cogs in her brain turned fast. She needed some help and – still holding the scroll in her hand – she reached for her phone.

'You're never going to believe this,' said Annabel.

'Good morning to you, too,' sounded Lucy's voice on the other end of the line.

'Sorry. Morning. It's just… I think my mother is up to something.

'What do you mean?'

'I had a delivery this morning.'

'From your mother?'

'Well, no. There was no sender, just a letter. But I can feel it. It was her.'

'What did she send you? Anything nice?'

'No— I mean… yes, I mean… no. Oh, God. It's an Advent calendar. It looks gorgeous.'

'That sounds lovely. What's the matter, then?'

'It's the message behind the window.'

'Message? There was no chocolate?'

'No. Just a message. Well, more like a task.'

'And what does it say?'

'I've just sent you a picture of it.'

'Oooh, you're right. This is devious.'

Sensing Lucy's tone, Annabel retorted. 'There's no need to be sarcastic, Lucy.'

'Oh, lighten up, Annabel. You don't even know it was her who sent it.'

'Who else could it be?'

'I don't know. What did the letter say?' asked Lucy.

Annabel read the letter to her friend, stopping at various points looking for confirmation that it was indeed her mother who was behind this and that it was all an act of manipulation.

'I thought your mum didn't like the Grinch?' responded Lucy.

Annabel sighed. 'No, she doesn't,' she said, with some resignation. 'But maybe that's just to put me off thinking that it was her.'

'So, what are you going to do?'

'I don't know. I need to find out if it was her.'

'So, you're going to go along with the task? It could be a bit of festive fun.'

'Fun? Do you not know me at all? Do you seriously think that my idea of fun is spending Christmas with the person who questions every decision I've ever made and who takes every opportunity to give her unsolicited advice no matter what the subject is? Really?'

'Don't get so worked up about it, Annabel. Every year you worry about this for weeks. You get yourself into a right state trying to work out how to get out of spending Christmas with your family. Wouldn't it be great if you just told them that this year, they've got their wish? With worrying out of the way you could get on with more important things.'

'But what about the part where I'd actually have to spend Christmas with them? Listening to my mother telling me how I've made a mistake moving down south and wanting to work in publishing all these years and how I could have had a great life if I stayed in Masham. She'll be keen to point out that I've never listened to her and now look where that got me. Nowhere. My life is a disaster. David left me and my career is a mess… if you can even call it a career.'

'Abi will be there, though,' said Lucy, trying to calm her friend's anxiety.

'That's even more reason for my mother to point out that at least one of her daughters has done well for herself. Abi and Hunter are planning their dream wedding. She was made partner at the local GP practice after Dr. Longbottom retired. Don't get me wrong, I love Abi dearly and I'm so happy for her but listening to my mother on repeat is no fun.'

'Well, maybe it won't be like that this year. Have you considered that? Maybe you could give it a chance.'

'You seem to be all for this idea. If you don't want me to spend Christmas with you, you could just say that,' she said, sulking.

'What are you talking about, Annabel? You know you're always welcome.'

'No, I get it. I've spent the last five Christmases with you guys and looking after the girls, the in-laws, and me on top of that is not easy. I was going to spend this Christmas with David and his family this year, but clearly that's not happening now. But that's not your problem. I shouldn't expect you to take me in every time I have a wobble.'

'Please just stop, Annabel. You know that me and Hugh love having you around for Christmas. And the kids are always so excited about you joining us. You are always welcome here; you don't even have to ask. But don't you think it's time you sorted things out with your mother? It's gone on for far too long. I think you'll feel so much better once you've talked things over. Maybe you could give it a shot and play along. What do you think?'

Annabel went quiet for a few seconds.

'I hope there's a treat somewhere behind these windows if I'm doing this,' she replied, still sulking.

'That's the spirit. I've got to go now. Nelly is hosting an Advent party for her dolls and teddies and I'm baking the biscuits. I'll call you later.'

With the phone still in one hand and the scroll in the other, she recalled the message that fell from behind the little window marked with number one. If it wasn't her worst nightmare, it was pretty close. But she was no quitter and as much as she hated to admit, Lucy was right. She had tried to ignore these issues for a long time and maybe it was time she started facing things.

The phone in her hand, she scanned her spotless kitchen for a bowl or spoon she forgot to wash after her elaborate breakfast. But the countertop was completely clear. Not a cup or plate in sight. She'd even tidied away all the items from the draining board. It had been over an hour since she'd hung up the phone with Lucy.

'Come on, Annabel. You'll feel much better once it's done,' she told herself as she re-read the message.

Arrange to spend Christmas with your family

With everything looking spic and span, she surrendered: she couldn't put the call off any longer. The sweet scent of banana pancakes still lingered in the room as she scrolled through her contacts, hovering her finger over the call button.

'Let's do this,' she said, exhaling sharply.

The phone rang and rang, and she was almost ready to hang up when an exasperated voice greeted her on the other side.

'Darling, what a nice surprise!' Evelyn answered, still slightly out of breath.

Annabel wasn't convinced that what she was about to say was a good idea, but mentally she had committed to the challenge.

'Just called to see if you had room for one more this Christmas?' she asked, her heart pounding in her throat.

'Of course, we do. Why?'

'I was thinking about coming home for the holidays.'

'Really? That's such wonderful news. It'll be great to have you here. Is David coming along, too?'

Annabel hesitated. 'No. It'll only be me.'

'Oh, that's a shame. Is everything all right?'

'Yeah, everything's fine.'

After a few more awkward questions she managed to cut the conversation short.

'I've got to go, Mum,' she said before hanging up the phone.

Her mother was clearly pleased that Annabel had decided to join them for Christmas. Annabel, on the other hand, wasn't so sure she could share her enthusiasm. But she promised she'd go, so there was no going back.

The next morning, Annabel wasn't in a hurry to get up. Sunday lie-ins didn't happen often. She either had work to do or errands to run, so she was determined to make the most of this rare opportunity. Besides, the cold, dark winter mornings weren't exactly the encouragement anyone needed to get out of bed. The cosy duvet was like a warm embrace. Comfort even on the harshest of days.

Her thoughts turned to yesterday's events and her conversation with her mother. It almost seemed like a dream, and she still couldn't quite believe that she would be spending Christmas with her family. She thought of many different scenarios about how things could play out and none of them were particularly pleasant, but it was all agreed and there was no going back now.

She quickly remembered the wooden box, and wondered what lay behind the second window. She hoped that it was something a bit more pleasant, but based on the task the day before she couldn't be sure.

As much as she enjoyed the idle morning, she wasn't good at staying put for long. After a quick glance at her bedside alarm clock, she reluctantly flung the covers off.

Throwing her dressing gown over her pyjamas, she headed to the kitchen. Five minutes later the smell of coffee wafted across the living room like it did every morning. She found comfort in the familiar scent that signalled the start of a new day. It was her private ritual, her time to feel present and grounded before she got swept up in the madness of life.

The wooden box stood on the dining table. Usually a nest of treasures, the forebearer of the festivities to come. But what would it hold for Annabel?

She pulled out one of the chairs and sat down, placing her cup on the table. She scanned the windows, looking for number two until her eyes rested on it. She hesitated for a moment before opening the tiny hatch. She took out the scroll and took a sip of coffee before unrolling it, not sure what to expect.

Try a new group class

Annabel felt her whole body soften as she read the message. The weather looked grim outside, and she was determined not to leave her flat; so, the task posed a bit of an inconvenience.

But thinking back to yesterday's challenge, this would be a breeze. A few minutes later she found herself scrolling through her local fitness centre's website.

It was five minutes before the class was about to start when Annabel arrived at the studio. The place wasn't full, but many had already taken their place in the room. She glanced at the participants, trying to judge the level of physical torment she might be subjected to. Guessing that the average age was around forty to forty-five she thought, *I'm sure I'll be all right.* But she didn't want to leave things to chance, so she positioned her mat at the back of the room away from the first line of scrutiny.

Just as she was about to settle the instructor arrived, full of energy and enthusiasm.

'How are we doing, ladies? We'll be doing some dumbbell exercises today, if you want to grab a couple before we get started.'

Annabel could feel her body freeze as her eyes stopped on the instructor. She was grateful that she was at the back of the room, but as the others flocked to gather the weights Annabel quickly followed their lead. There were no instructions on the weight, and while most had picked up a pair of two-kilo ones, some had gone for heavier three-kilo weights.

Annabel hesitated, her eyes darting from the weights to the instructor anxiously. Not wanting to be the last one to leave, she quickly grabbed a pair of three-kilo dumbbells.

'We'll change things up a bit today,' said the smooth voice as he walked to the back of the studio. 'Let's all turn to face the back of the room.'

Annabel felt her legs weaken as Alex stood only a couple of meters away from her. She fiddled with her shoelaces, desperately trying to avoid eye contact.

'It's nice to see some familiar faces,' Alex said, glancing briefly around the room before smiling at Annabel.

All the blood rushed to her cheeks.

'Let's start with a warm up,' he suggested.

The initial breathing exercises felt nice and easy, and Annabel's muscle tension started to ease somewhat. A few minutes in and after a series of gentle movements, she started to feel a little less self-conscious.

I can do this, she thought.

But the pace soon picked up and the dumbbells were put to use. Alex's commanding voice bounced off the walls of the studio. 'Five, four, three, two, one. Great job, ladies. Thirty seconds rest.'

She regretted picking three-kilo weights.

The instructions kept coming and by the time she was at the end of the third round of squats and jumping jacks, she felt like the final fifteen seconds were never going to end. Sweat trickled down her forehead as they held the plank for the third time during that class. Holding the position for sixty seconds didn't seem like too long at first, but after two rounds she wasn't sure how much more her body could take.

She stared at her watch as it lit up, her pulse racing. Halfway through her upper arms started to shake, and a few seconds later she was close to dropping to her knees.

Oh, God. I can't be the first one to drop, she thought.

She didn't know how, but somehow she managed to hold up her body nearly to the end of the minute. Her arms felt like jelly and all she wanted was to collapse on the floor.

'Well done, ladies,' boomed Alex's voice. 'That was the last one for today.'

Annabel was relieved the torment was over, her pulse slowing and her breath returning to its natural rhythm.

'He's great, isn't he?' chimed one of the ladies next to her as she put away the dumbbells. She must have been a good ten years older than Annabel, but her cheeks were barely pink, and only a faint shimmer of sweat on her forehead.

'Terrific,' Annabel managed. 'Is it always this fast-paced?'

'Oh yeah. That's why we come,' replied the woman with a huge smile.

Annabel looked around and Alex seemed to be busy chatting to a couple of women. She was keen to slip away unnoticed, so keeping her eyes firmly on the door, she headed towards it.

'I think you forgot something,' came Alex's voice as she reached for the door handle. She looked back. The women Alex had been talking to were headed in her direction; Alex stood a few metres away, her water bottle in his hand. She could feel her heart rate accelerate once again and heat returned to her cheeks. She knew they were glowing red.

'Thanks.' She managed a faint smile.

'Isabel, is it?' asked Alex.

'Annabel.'

'Oh, that's right. It's nice to see you again. How did you like the class?'

'It was very...,' she paused. 'Invigorating,' she said, after some hesitation.

'Glad you enjoyed it.' Alex smiled.

Enjoyment wasn't the first thing that came to Annabel's mind. Conscious of her sweat-soaked attire and her flushed complexion, she felt more and more uncomfortable standing there.

'Thanks,' she said, taking the water bottle from Alex's outstretched hand. 'I'd better get going now.'

'Sure. Hope to see you around again,' said Alex, before Annabel swung the door open and hurried in the direction of the changing rooms.

The aftereffects of the previous night's exercise class really started to intensify as the morning went on. Annabel concluded that she might have been a bit too ambitious thinking that she could handle full body fusion. She had to admit that her current level of fitness was more suited to tai-chi. At least she was glad she didn't go for Insanity. *That would have probably killed me*, she thought. She was aching in places she didn't know she could, and she still felt slightly embarrassed that she couldn't keep up with the seventy-year-old woman in the front row, and mortified that all this had played out in front of Alex.

She shivered and shook her head in an attempt to clear the memory. *Why was he there?* she contemplated. *I thought he said he was an actor.* Swallowed up in a cloud of embarrassment, she never thought to ask what he was doing there. She attempted to reclaim some calm from the voice of her bruised ego and her thoughts turned to the piece of paper in her hand. It was the day's note from the wooden box.

The task sounded simple enough, but after the events of the last two days she wasn't convinced that continuing with the tasks was a good idea. Besides, she knew she could easily be roped into something she usually made great efforts to stay away from. Not ready to decide, she tucked the piece of paper into her folder after reading it one more time.

It was the kick-off meeting for the new project and Sandra was already in the meeting room talking to Thomas, the Marketing Director, when Annabel arrived.

'Can't wait to get started,' Sandra exclaimed, as Annabel took her seat at the table.

Annabel laid out her notes as Sandra opened the meeting. It soon became apparent that Sandra wasn't shying away from being the centre of attention.

'I'm so excited to be leading this project. I know we have a good team and under my strong direction, this will no doubt be a huge success. But we have a lot to do and a tight deadline to meet, so it's really all hands on deck,' said Sandra, her voice commanding. 'As you all know, we will be working on *My Face in the Mirror.* We estimate 6 months to publication.'

'Six months?' asked Ben surprised.

'Yes. That's the aim. But we might be able to complete even sooner than that,' replied Sandra. 'I have already finished the first round of developmental edits and based on my initial notes we will need at least another round to finalise the details of the changes required. The premise of Avery infiltrating a Russian underground organisation is great, but I think the focus is too much on how he battles with his personal demons. It's a bit on the soft side and I think it makes the story less pacey. So, I suggest that we shift the focus more to the inner workings of the organisation and toughen Avery up a bit.'

Liv chuckled to herself, and Annabel shot her concerned look. But she had to agree, she couldn't imagine Sandra toughening anyone up either.

'Did I say something funny?' asked Sandra, her eyes a blaze.

'No, sorry, it's just my allergy. It's been bothering my throat all morning,' said Liv with conviction.

'Oh. Well, you might want to get some of that nasal spray. It's supposed to be good, I heard,' replied Sandra, her face softening slightly.

'Has Mr Shaw agreed to the changes?' asked Annabel slightly concerned.

'Not yet. But we should be in receipt of his signed contract any day and I'm sure he will be more than happy to incorporate the necessary changes,' replied Sandra.

A prickling sensation spread across the back of Annabel's neck. She hated the idea of ripping the main character's personality away and replacing it with a shallower one just for the sake of commercialism. The main reason she felt so strongly about Shaw's manuscript was the grittiness of Avery's struggle and the question of whether he could remain his true self or if he would be swallowed up by the cold and merciless world around him. Annabel's eyes fixed on her notes; she knew if she lifted her gaze to meet Sandra's, she would find it extremely hard to control her words.

'So you're suggesting making the story a bit more James Bond-esque?' she said quietly.

'Well, a bit more masculine, if that's what you're referring to,' replied Sandra curtly. 'Do you have anything against that?'

Annabel lifted her gaze to meet Sandra's. She could sense that her own viewpoint would not be welcome, so she decided to take a more tactical path. 'Well, it's just that would change the story quite drastically. Not sure how Mr Shaw feels about that. Plus, it could take a long time to rewrite. With the tight deadline, that might be quite a task.'

'Mr Shaw is open to changes and I'm sure he'll be happy to rewrite the manuscript based on our feedback. At the end of the day, we know what sells and it can be a great story, but if it doesn't sell, there's not much point writing it. So, we have to make it the best we think it can be. And, yes, I'm aware that it will take some doing, but I know you are all up to the task. I'll share the details with you Annabel and you can start working on the second round of developmental edits on that basis. Once you have a draft, I'll take a look at it.' replied Sandra, her teeth glinting in the sunshine that streamed in through the window.

The rest of the meeting was spent with Sandra drawing a timeline up for each piece of work to be done and allocating tasks to everyone but herself. She was at the 'top of the pyramid' as she said, so once all the workstreams had been completed under her close supervision she would bring it all together. Annabel didn't like the direction one bit but she didn't know how she could change Sandra's mind on turning the manuscript into a mass market pulp fiction.

As everyone was leaving the room after the meeting, Thomas stayed behind to find out how the preparations for the Christmas party were progressing. Sandra replied with great enthusiasm.

'Everything is coming together really nicely. The caterers sent me the menu, and everyone has chosen their meals. The band has confirmed as well and I'm due to go down there next week to check on the decorations. Everything is under control.' She beamed at him.

'Although,' she continued, with a slight disappointment in her voice, 'Eloise pulled out of helping with the set up so I need to find someone else who can assist me.'

Annabel was just gathering her things ready to head back to her desk when the note fell out of her folder. She picked up the piece of paper and unfolded it, taking another look.

Volunteer to help out on a project at work

Despite her apprehension before taking on each task, she felt strangely satisfied that she had completed the first two assignments in the calendar, and she felt a little uncomfortable at the thought that she might fail on the third day. *What would have been the point of agreeing to spend Christmas with Mum and making a fool of myself in front of Alex if I stopped here?* But the thought of spending more time with Sandra filled her with dread. Having to work with her on this new project was hard as it was, and she wasn't sure she could take any more of Sandra's exaggerated enthusiasm. But Annabel couldn't ignore that this might be the perfect opportunity to complete the day's challenge. *Maybe this could provide a chance to persuade Sandra to change her mind on the direction of this project,* thought Annabel as she approached them.

'I didn't mean to eavesdrop, but I heard you're in need of extra help with the Christmas party prep.'

'Yes, Eloise's parents are in town for the next week and it's not often they come. She wanted to spend as much time with them as she could, so she had to pull out. There's a lot to get ready and I could really do with an extra pair of hands. I'd be over the moon if you could help,' replied Sandra with her usual over-the-top enthusiasm.

Annabel didn't reply for a moment, already second guessing her earlier choice.

Sensing Annabel's hesitation Sandra quickly added:

'Even if you can just give me a hand for an hour, it would great help. You can finish early that day, too.'

Annabel scrunched up the note in her hand as she replied. 'Let me know the details and I'm sure I can make myself available.'

As she left the room, she was pleased to have completed the challenge, but soon her contentment turned into slight unease at the thought of spending time with Sandra outside of work. She wasn't completely over getting pipped to the post by her on the interview, and spending a whole afternoon together might not be the best cure.

Chapter 3

Start reading a new book. One you'd never pick off the shelf

One might assume this was one of the easiest tasks she could have been given, but for Annabel it wasn't so. She loved to read and so naturally every book she owned was one she'd love to read if she hadn't already. So, going through her bookshelf would be no use.

Throughout the day she struck up conversations with colleagues to see what they were reading and whether she'd find something she wouldn't normally go for. Without much luck, she decided to go by the bookshop on her way home and buy Kawaguchi's book for next month's event.

She could have gone to Waterstones down the road, but she wanted something intriguing to read. It had been a while since she visited Bibliophilia, an independent bookshop on Richmond's high street. The bookshelves were arranged in a curve, snaking around the room and luring you further and further in. Coming to this place always felt like entering a labyrinth with the hope of finding treasure at the end, which she often did. The smell of antique and new books mixing with the lingering aroma of hot coffee and baked goods was strangely comforting.

It was easy to lose track of time and get lost in the maze or find herself in one of the reading pods hanging in a quiet corner like colourful chrysalises. Besides, Santiago, the shop's owner, always had some good recommendations up his sleeve.

Browsing the contemporary fiction section, she soon found Before the Coffee Gets Cold. She stepped back from the shelf only to walk straight into the path of the man passing behind her, nearly knocking a book out of his hand. She started to apologise when she noticed who the man was.

'Oh. Hi, Alex,' she said, her voice cracking slightly.

'And we meet again. Ariel, right?'

'It's Annabel,' she replied.

'Of course. Sorry, I meet a lot of people and names can get a bit muddled up,' he added. 'I'm starting to think that you might be stalking me,' he said with a smile.

Annabel's face turned red.

'I wouldn't be offended if you were,' he added quickly.

'I could say the same,' retorted Annabel, returning the smile. 'I mean that you might be stalking me, not that I wouldn't be offended.' Her cheeks felt increasingly warm. 'Do you live around here?' As soon as the words left her mouth, she felt awkward. She didn't want to sound like she was prying. 'I mean, do you come here a lot?'

'Oh, no. I live in the city. Just came to pick this up.' He raised the book in his hand.

'*Haikus on Death*,' he said.

An interesting choice, she thought. 'Are you a fan of Japanese poetry?'

'Yeah, you could say that. I write a bit myself,' he added, casually.

'You seem to be a man of many talents,' observed Annabel. 'I thought you were an actor, so it kind of threw me when you turned up at the class the other day.'

'I am. Fitness is another passion of mine and a friend mentioned they were thinking about adding a new class to the timetable, so I thought this would be great. And they love it.'

'Well, it seems popular, for sure.'

'Hope you didn't feel too drained afterwards.'

'Oh, no. It was great,' said Annabel, without conviction.

'So are you looking for anything in particular?' he asked, pointing to the shelves.

'Nothing in particular, but *Haikus on Death* sounds interesting. I was looking for something different and I think I might have found it. Are you coming along next week?' she asked, before quickly adding, 'To the book club?'

She felt her cheeks turn pink again as she waited for his answer, but he didn't seem to notice Annabel's nerves.

'I've got quite a lot on at the theatre at the moment, but I liked the discussion last time.'

'Maybe I'll see you there, then.' Sensing their conversation had run its natural course, she made her excuses and headed to the poetry section. Thoughts swirled in her head about how dreamy he was and how much of a fool she has made of herself once again, she trawled through the shelves searching for *Haikus on Death.*

Santiago was at the till serving customers when she got there. 'Annabel! What a great surprise! It's been a while since I last saw you here.'

Although there were plenty of other shop assistants around, Santiago liked to get involved and have a chat with people visiting his shop.

'I know. It's been a busy couple of months, but it's always nice to come down here and have a look around,' she replied, placing the book on the counter.

'Not your usual choice,' said Santiago.

'No. I thought I'd try something different.'

'Was it a recommendation?' he asked as he turned the book to scan it.

'Sort of.'

'Well, do tell me what it's like when you're next in.'

After a long day, Annabel was glad she'd completed her task, but she wasn't sure she was in the mood for poems on death.

***

Most days, Annabel had a good routine of waking at the same time without the need for an alarm. But when it went off the next morning, she wasn't ready to rise. Still in the middle of a dream, it took her a minute or so to register the loud buzzing noise coming from her bedside. She let out a short groan as Marley leapt onto the bed, trying to get her attention.

Images played in her head like scenes on a black-and-white movie reel. They seemed vivid and rather strange. She remembered running across some dark woods under the moonlight. Her feet felt cold on the ground. She couldn't recall her dreams very often, but when she had a particularly strange one, she often shared it with David. He never really seemed to listen or engage in a conversation about them. 'I don't think it means anything. It must have been something you've read last night,' he often said. But the thought of not having someone to share her wonderings with made Annabel sad.

Not wanting to be caught in the sticky trap of self-pity or analyse too much what her subconscious might be trying to tell her, she decided it was time to get up. As she flung the covers aside, a thud made Marley flinch. She looked around to see a book lying on the floor.

'The dream makes a bit more sense now, I suppose,' she concluded, picking it up.

She wasn't convinced that it was her sort of thing after all and wondered if she could swap it for something a bit less intense next time. *I'm sure Santiago wouldn't mind.*

Her phone beeped, bringing her back to the present.

'Typical,' she said, feeling annoyed she scanned through the email.

The weekly editorial review meeting had been brought forward to nine and she still had some prep to do beforehand. She had to be out of the door in fifteen minutes to catch her train, if she was going to make it.

Thankfully, Annabel was a master of working quickly in time-pressured situations and by half past seven she was on her way to the city. She had twenty-five minutes to go over her notes and plan for the day ahead. Things were under control once again, but she had a nagging feeling that she had forgotten something in her haste. She checked her pocket for her phone relieved to find it there. *Did I lock the door?* She was positive that she did. She couldn't think what she might have missed, so she tried to reassure herself that it must be nothing.

'What's up with you?' asked Liv as they walked back to their desks. 'You've been quiet all morning.'

'I didn't sleep well last night, and I keep thinking I forgot something this morning.'

'Is working with *her* getting to you already? I wouldn't blame you if it did.'

'No, it's not that. Just had some weird dreams.'

'Ooh, anything saucy?'

'Leave it out, Liv. Don't have any mental energy for that kind of stuff.'

'You're not still hung up on David, are you?'

'No.'

'That wasn't very convincing.'

'It's not David. But it would be nice to be missed or greeted by anyone else other than Marley.'

Liv wrapped an arm around Annabel. 'You'll meet someone great, I'm sure of that and until then, enjoy the single life.'

'Thanks, Liv,' replied Annabel, batting the thoughts away. 'Besides, I've got other things to worry about. Like this project and Sandra's crazy ideas. I need to find a way to make her see sense.'

'Good luck with that,' said Liv. 'Here, you can open the window on my Advent calendar today. You deserve a little sugar boost.'

'The calendar,' mumbled Annabel. In her hurry, she'd forgotten to open the day's window on the Advent calendar.

'What?' asked Liv.

'Nothing, I just realised what I'd forgotten.'

She checked her watch. She thought she might have time to go back during her lunch, but with back-to-back meetings all day, that wouldn't be possible. Reluctantly, she accepted that she might have to wait until the evening.

The whole day, Annabel tried to guess what the message behind the window might be and who sent her the mysterious gift. Her suspicions were still firmly on her mother.

The hours ticked by, and she found herself stressing more and more that she might not have time to complete the task. As she sat on the train heading home, her ideas getting wilder and wilder about the contents of the Advent calendar, until the beep of her phone brought her back to reality.

Haven't seen you in a while. Hope you're not still down in the dumps and that you aren't mad at me for what I said.

She hadn't spoken to James for a few days, but not because she took offence at his advice. Life just seemed to have got in the way.

She quickly typed out a reply:

Sorry… Not mad, just been busy. And thanks for asking, feeling a bit better. I still owe you dinner though.

As she hit send, a thought occurred to her: *could James have sent the calendar? He thought I wouldn't listen and maybe this was his plan B.* Annabel sunk deep in thought, and soon came James's reply:

Glad to hear that. No worries. Just drop me a text if you feel up for grabbing some food x

Trying to get rid of the nagging though Annabel typed out another message before deleting it. *It won't hurt if I ask*, she thought re-typing the text.

Will do. Did you send me a parcel, by any chance??

She waited nervously before the screen flashed up again.

No. Should I have? I thought your birthday wasn't until spring.

Slightly disappointed, Annabel replied:

No. Just got a delivery with no sender details. It was probably my mother…

As soon as she got home, she headed straight to the box. Keen to see what lay behind the window of number five, she unrolled the scroll.

Buy tickets for a show or concert

Her first reaction was relief. The task seemed manageable in the amount of time she still had left.

'A show or a concert,' she repeated. She tried to recall the last time she went to the theatre or saw a band play live. It might have been a stand-up comedy act, but the details were hazy. *Clearly, it wasn't one to remember.*

She scrolled through the events listings for a while, but without much luck. A couple of pantomimes, a few Christmas concerts, but nothing that grabbed her attention. Marley jumped on the table with a loud meow. He hasn't been impressed with being ignored lately and he was determined to make his views heard. He sat down on the table right next to the Advent calendar, carrying on, demanding her attention.

Annabel glanced at the box. Staring at the painted picture, she realised what she was looking for. Some minutes later she was the proud owner of two tickets for Saturday night.

She remembered visiting the theatre as a child with her mother and being mesmerised by the costumes and the set. The dancing figures drew her into their world. Besides, she couldn't think of many other things that reminded her more of Christmas than The Nutcracker.

The next morning, Annabel made sure she didn't forget to open number six on the Advent calendar before heading out for the day. But her enthusiasm was short lived as she read the text. Unease settled in the pit of her stomach, and she was even more convinced than before who was behind her gift. She made great efforts throughout the day to bury her head in work and was doing great until four o'clock that afternoon. She left work early and with Marley in the carrier, she headed to the vet a couple of streets away from her flat.

Mrs Sharp was sat at reception when she got there. Her glasses slid down her nose and she peered over them when she heard Annabel approach the desk.

'Good afternoon. I've got an appointment with Mr Ito at four for Marley's checkup,' said Annabel.

'Let me see,' replied Mrs Sharp, turning back to her computer screen. 'Oh yes, there it is. Mr Ito is on time today. You won't have to wait too long. If you'd like to take a seat over there, Miss Tate. I'll call you when he's ready.' Mrs Sharp pointed at a seat in the far corner, away from the Great Dane waiting for his turn. Always keeping things under control, she ran the practice like a military operation.

Mrs Sharp had worked at Mr Ito's practice for a couple of years. Always punctual, she never missed a day of work. She had worked as a headmistress for the local secondary school before retiring about five years ago. When her husband passed away suddenly, she decided to come out of retirement. She was the kind of person whose mere presence commanded respect. It wasn't long before Mrs Sharp called her.

'Mr Ito is ready for you now, Miss Tate.'

As Annabel entered the room, Mr Ito was getting his instruments ready for the exam.

'Good to see you, Marley,' he greeted the box's unhappy occupant. 'And of course, it's nice to see you again, Annabel. How's Marley been?'

'He's been doing well, thank you. His appetite returned pretty quickly after the treatment last time, and he seems to be back to his usual self.'

A couple of months back, Marley wasn't eating and didn't seem his usual playful self. When he didn't improve, Annabel had started to worry. She rushed down to the vet practice one night, hoping to find Mr Ito there. It was after closing time, but he often stayed longer, and Annabel was in luck that day. After a quick examination, he found the root of the problem: an infected tooth. An antibiotic shot and a couple of days of medication seemed to have done the trick. Annabel couldn't have been more grateful, but Mr Ito wouldn't accept any extra payment for the out-of-hours work other than his usual rate and the cost of the medication. He was passionate about his profession and although he treated injuries and ailments of many kinds in different animals, he had a real soft spot for cats.

'That's great to hear. We will take a look at that tooth today just to make sure it won't bother him again,' he said.

As she waited, Annabel noticed that the only photo hung on Mr Ito's wall was one of a rather grumpy-looking cat. She wondered why there were no pictures of a family anywhere, but perhaps Mr Ito's dedication to his patients and the long days at the surgery were clues to the answer. Annabel wondered for a moment if he was happy with the choices he'd made, dedicating his life to his career. But she knew it wasn't her place to question that, even if it was only to herself.

'Is he yours?' she asked, gesturing towards the picture.

'He was,' said Mr Ito.

'I'm so sorry. I didn't realise,' said Annabel.

'Don't worry,' replied Mr Ito quickly with a smile. 'It was a long time ago. Kitaro was a great companion, and I haven't met one like him since.'

'I know what you mean,' said Annabel, looking at Marley.

After a thorough examination and with his vaccination complete, Marley was given the 'all clear' along with one of his favourite treats, which seemed to make up for some of his unhappiness.

'He is in good health,' said Mr Ito, turning to Annabel. 'Provided he behaves himself, I shouldn't need to see him for another year.'

'That's great news. Thank you, Mr Ito.'

Marley was keen to get back into the safety of his box, ready to head home.

Before heading upstairs, Annabel went to check her letterbox, although she wasn't expecting much other than a few takeaway leaflets. But as she opened the letterbox, a cream-coloured envelope fell to the floor. She eagerly opened it, revealing the tickets to Saturday's show. *That was fast*, she thought. For the last hour, she had managed to put the task out of her mind, but the tickets reminded her that she had unfinished business.

An elderly man came through the door just as she closed the letter box. She had seen him around before, but they'd never said more than a few words to each other. Today seemed no different. He nodded his head towards her before making his way to the stairs. As he walked past Annabel, an envelope dropped to the floor and he didn't seem to notice. She picked it up, wanting to call after him, but she realised she didn't know his name. She quickly turned the letter over.

'Mr Adler,' she called, but he didn't seem to hear. She gathered her post and Marley's box and rushed after the man, tapping him on the shoulder. Slightly startled, he turned around.

'Mr Adler, you've dropped this,' she said as she held out the letter.

'Oh, thank you, Miss...'

'I'm Annabel. I live at number twenty.'

'Nice to meet you, Annabel. Sorry, but my hearing is not all that great,' he replied, pointing at the device in his ear.

'Don't worry,' said Annabel with a smile. 'I better get going. He wants to be let out,' she said lifting Marley's box slightly. 'It was lovely to meet you, Mr Adler. I'm sure I'll see you around.'

Once she let Marley out and put the pet carrier away, the cat's unease seemed to let up a bit. She placed the tickets on the table and searched in her pocket for the day's task just to check it again.

Arrange to spend quality time with your mother

Thinking back to the first task, she felt a sense of discomfort. *If I could do that first task, surely this one shouldn't be a problem.* But this was different. With others around at Christmas, her mother would have other things on her mind and the spotlight wouldn't fall on Annabel solely. With just the two of them, there was nowhere to hide from the scrutiny of her mother's questions. Amongst her angst, she could still hear Lucy's words: *you have to sort this out with your mother.* She couldn't fail at the fifth task. Everything she'd done so far would have been for nothing. Her palms were warm and clammy. Her heart was beating faster. With a deep inhale, she took her phone out and dialled before she could change her mind.

'Hello,' said George.

'Hi, Dad. It's Annabel.'

'Oh, hi, duck. Good to hear your voice. How are you doing?'

'I'm doing well, Dad. Just been to the vet with Marley.'

'What's up with him now?'

'Nothing, just his annual checkup. He's fine.'

'That's good, then. I thought he might have been causing some trouble again. Your mother said you'll be joining us for Christmas. It'll be nice to have you here.'

'Yes, I'm looking forward to it. I'll come up on the twenty-fourth and help with the prep.'

'Your mother will like that. She's always insistent on doing everything herself, but I'm sure she'll appreciate the help.'

'Speaking of which, is Mum around?'

'Yes, she's just in the kitchen making a cuppa. Hang on a minute. Evelyn!' he shouted. 'Annabel's on the phone.'

Annabel could hear Howler barking in the background at the mention of her name.

'She's coming now. I'll see you soon, duck,' he said, before passing the phone to his wife.

'Hello, darling,' said Evelyn. 'What a nice surprise, two calls in a week. What's the occasion?'

'Hi, Mum. Nothing, just calling to see how you are.'

'That's nice. But nothing exciting has been happening here. I have a feeling though, that you didn't call to hear about my day.'

'No. I…' Annabel hesitated.

'Is there something wrong?'

'No. I wanted to see if you're free on Saturday.'

'I should be. Why do you ask?'

'I've got a couple of tickets to The Nutcracker and thought you might want to come along with me to see it.'

'The Nutcracker! I haven't seen that show for years,' she said. 'I was planning on coming up to the city at some point. Still got a bit of shopping to do before Christmas and it would be lovely to see you, too. We could get some lunch before and make a day of it.'

'Sure. Sounds good. I'll text you the details and I can meet you at the station.'

'Looking forward to it, darling. See you on Saturday,' replied Evelyn.

As Annabel hung up the phone, she felt the fizzing sensation return to her stomach, spreading the unease. She should have been content that her task was complete, but she couldn't shake the thought that the day might end in disaster.

Chapter 4

'Good morning, Annabel,' Sandra greeted her when she arrived at work the following day. 'Are you going to be okay leaving at four this afternoon?' she asked.

Puzzled, Annabel didn't answer for a second.

'I hope you can still help out with the Christmas party preparations,' Sandra continued.

The question suddenly made sense. Annabel had completely forgotten about her offer the other day to help with the arrangements.

'Of course,' she said quickly. 'I forgot what day it was for a second, but I'll be ready to leave at four.'

Sandra was often about as subtle as a hurricane. She didn't do reserved. Wherever she turned up, she was sure to leave lasting memories. They couldn't have been more different, and Annabel wasn't exactly relishing the thought of one-on-one time with her, but she'd made a promise, and she was determined to face the challenge with her usual positive attitude.

She also had a slight ulterior motive: she thought that by helping Sandra out, she might be able to convince her to keep the core premise of Shaw's manuscript intact. She had her work cut out, but she had never shied away from a challenge.

As they got to the venue Sandra went through the to-do list.

'Right, we've got the decorations to haul in once the delivery van arrives, and we need to finalise the seating plan and sort where everything is going. There's quite a bit to do, but I'm sure we'll get through the list in no time,' said Sandra confidently.

'Sure, just let me know where to start,' replied Annabel just as the van pulled up outside.

It took about an hour to haul everything in and arrange the boxes in the storage area. Annabel had to admire Sandra's planning skills. She certainly thought of everything. Every box was strategically placed and labelled, making it easy to find where everything was. Sandra looked pleased with the work they've done.

'That's one job done.'

'I'm sure it's going to be a great party with all this work you've put in. You really have a knack for organising everything,' said Annabel.

'This is nothing. I used to work for an event planning company, and we'd organise events for hundreds of people at a time. I really enjoyed it.'

'I see. So what made you change direction to publishing?' asked Annabel as they slotted the last couple of boxes into place.

'I loved working in events, but after a while it got a bit samey. I was looking for something different and I ended up getting a role at a magazine through a friend. I'd worked there for a year or so when I heard that Herold & Hains was looking for an editorial assistant and I thought, "Why not?" I applied, had my interview with Thomas and the rest is history, as they say,' she said, laughing. 'How about you?'

'Me? Well, I've only ever worked in publishing. It was kind of a dream of mine ever since I was a young girl. I know it's silly, really,' said Annabel, feeling conscious that she'd never opened up like that to Sandra before.

'Not at all. It must be great to have such a strong focus.'

'It is and it isn't. It can get frustrating when progress is slow.'

'So, you've been at Herold & Hains for a few years, right?'

'Yeah, eight years. I got a job here soon after leaving uni and I've been here ever since.'

Sandra sat quiet for a moment. 'That must have been hard, then, when they gave the job to me.'

A knot gathered in Annabel's throat, and she had to take a deep breath and swallow before she replied. 'I was disappointed, sure,' she said, pausing. 'But you've clearly done a great job and I got over it.'

'Well, you're clearly a better person than me. I would have been fuming,' Sandra said with a laugh.

'Well, I still get to work on the project so that's a win,' said Annabel, trying not to sound bitter. 'Speaking of the project, I was thinking about the new direction for the Shaw manuscript, and I was wondering how set on it are you?' asked Annabel, hoping that Sandra was in a mood to hear her out.

'You mean the core changes?' asked Sandra.

Annabel nodded silently.

'Look, I know you took a liking to the original concept, but we had a discussion at a senior level, and it just makes more financial sense to change it. It's still a great story, but we have to think with a commercial mind. What's the point of publishing it if it won't sell?'

'So…' started Annabel hesitantly. 'If I could show you that it could be viable without the change, you'd think about it?'

'Maybe. But we have a tight deadline and you have loads to do as it is. You don't need any extra work thinking about this avenue. You might just have to let this one go.' Sandra's tone made the hairs on Annabel's neck stand up. 'We'd better get on with this seating plan. Speaking of which, I don't think I've seen your name on the list, Annabel. Are you not coming?'

'I wasn't going to. I had some other plans next weekend,' she replied.

'That's such a shame. You could come for the dinner at least, and stay for a bit if you need to get back early,' said Sandra. 'You could bring your boyfriend along, too. There are still some spare tickets left.'

'Oh, we broke up a few weeks ago,' replied Annabel.

'Oh, that's such a shame. Well, still, have a think about it. It will be great fun.'

'Maybe,' said Annabel reluctantly.

'It's really promising to be a great night. The jazz band has confirmed, and they are amazing. I saw them a couple of months back in a bar in Soho and I knew they would be perfect for this party. And there's also a free bar,' she added with a cheeky grin.

Annabel was partial to a nice glass of white wine now and then, but she wasn't much of a drinker and the thought of unlimited alcohol consumption wasn't exactly high on her list of priorities. Besides, she could see how things might go downhill after a few hours. When she joined Herold & Hains she attended the Christmas party that year, but ever since then she made great efforts to avoid these get togethers. She wanted to keep her professional life separate from her personal one. Bonding with your boss in a booze-filled state worked for some, but Annabel felt it could ruin the professional image she worked hard to maintain. As she thought of more reasons for not attending, she remembered the day's challenge.

Say yes to something you'd normally say no to

Attending the office Christmas party was definitely one of those things she'd automatically reject and despite every bone in her body screaming it was a bad idea, she agreed to go along.

'The band sounds great,' she said. 'Maybe I could come for a bit.'

'Great. You can sit next to me,' said Sandra.

Although she agreed to come along, Annabel intended to leave before any awkward encounters. Just as they started to sort out the seating plan, Thomas arrived.

'Good afternoon, ladies,' he greeted them.

'Oh, hi, Thomas. Didn't expect to see you here,' said Sandra.

'I was just in the area and thought I'd pop in to see how things were going.'

'We've made great progress. We've still got the seating plan to get through and a couple of other bits,' replied Sandra.

'I'm not in a rush, so I can give you a hand.'

Annabel smiled politely at this offer. She wasn't quite sure what it was about Thomas that made her uneasy. He was charming, approachable and seemed incredibly knowledgeable. When she thought about it, she couldn't remember ever seeing him on an off day. He always dressed impeccably, not a single speck of dust on his shoes. She didn't know why, but this apparent perfection somehow felt odd to her. *How can someone's shoes be so immaculate?* But there was no law against being too polished, and certainly no one could hold that against him as his only apparent flaw.

It took them an hour to sort out all hundred and fifty-five seats and finish everything, but by the end Sandra looked pleased.

'I can't believe it, but we've done it. It was great teamwork, guys. Thank you for offering to help, Annabel. Really appreciate it.'

'Don't mention it.'

'Yes, you've done an excellent job organising everything for next week,' said Thomas.

'Can't wait,' said Sandra. 'Do you guys want to grab some food, now we're all done here? There's a great Thai place just around the corner.'

'I love Thai food. I'm in,' replied Thomas without hesitation.

'Sounds good, but I'd better get off. It's been a long day. You enjoy the food though and I'll see you next week,' said Annabel. She was starting to warm to Sandra, but there was only so much of her over-the-top enthusiasm she could take for one day.

Feeling shattered, she collapsed in a heap on the sofa. As she looked around, the white walls made the room look painfully bare. It was nearly the second weekend of Advent and apart from the wooden box on the table, there was no sign of Christmas anywhere else in her flat. After hours of arranging party decorations, the lack of festive spirit in her apartment felt even more poignant. The little potted conifer stood lonely in the corner. She bought it last year as a trial to see if Marley would leave it alone, and it seemed to be resilient enough for the most part.

Looking at the tree, a thought occurred to her and she headed to the bedroom. She rattled through some boxes in the wardrobe before she finally found what she was looking for.

She dusted the lid off and opened it, revealing a treasure trove. The colours were rather subtle, reflective of Annabel's personality. She wasn't bold or loud. Most of the baubles were bronze rather than gold. She liked their earthy feel. Besides, somehow gold felt too obnoxious to her. Too brash. She came across some cream-coloured and emerald-green ribbons, a string of tangled fairy lights, a smaller box of wooden ornaments and the wreath that Lucy made her some years ago. By the time she finished unpacking the box, the contents covered half the floor around her.

Keen to get to work, Annabel headed back to the living room.

Despite Marley's interference, it didn't take her long to dress the tree and place a few decorations around the flat. She felt a sense of satisfaction as she lit the last tealight. The result was undoubtedly tasteful, but more importantly, she could feel herself getting into the spirit of Christmas.

***

It was Saturday morning and Annabel stood in front of her wardrobe with both doors wide open. Like many other people, she owned a number of garments that had been unloved for quite some time. They were bought with great enthusiasm at one point and worn once or twice, only to realise they didn't really suit her. She always had plans to wear them again another day, but old favourites had enjoyed priority over these pieces. Like the leather jacket she couldn't quite part with and had great visions for, or the broad-brimmed hat that was reminiscent of the one Audrey Hepburn wore in *Breakfast at Tiffany's*. Every time she wore it, she felt she was meant to do something glamorous, like going on a cruise or attending the races. Only she didn't like horse racing and got seasick every time she set foot on a boat, so she would convince herself that she couldn't pull off the look anyway. She read the piece of paper again she still held in her hand.

Donate unwanted possessions

The day's challenge served as a reason to have a good clear out and give away some of her unused possessions to a good cause. Besides, she had to find something to wear for the Christmas party, too.

Sliding the hangers to one side, she took out a couple of summer dresses. She held one in front of her as she surveyed her reflection.

'God, I can't remember the last time I wore this,' she mumbled to herself. *It must have been Nelly's Christening party,* she thought, putting the dress to one side.

A few more followed, ending up in a heap on the bed. 'I used to love this,' she exclaimed as she took another dress off the hanger. 'What do you think, Marley? Can I pull this off?' she asked as he ambled through the door, looking confused at the pile of clothes.

The moss-green dress hugged her hourglass figure; she kept tugging it down. Twirling in front of the mirror, a memory flashed through her mind. She closed her eyes as she remembered the music that vibrated through the hall.

It was her final year at university and the last day of exams was behind them. It was a hot summer evening, just her and the gang. They had no worries and very little care. She could still feel the euphoria she had felt dancing through the night.

Back then, the feeling that anything was possible was her true driving force; one that many admired her for. But as the memory of that night faded quickly, she felt she needed to peel this old skin away.

'It's just not me anymore,' she said, finally. The friendships that had seemed unbreakable had vanished over the years, her ambition now just a mirage she forever chased. She could feel a prickle of emotion rise in her throat as she sat on the bed. Quickly realising that she was rapidly descending on this spiral, she grabbed the garment and folded it a couple of times. She stuffed it at the bottom of the donation box; attempting to stifle the throbbing ache in her chest.

She spent another hour trawling through her possessions, parading in various outfits until she had managed to part with a boxful of clothes.

'I think I'll keep this one,' she said as she pulled on the last garment. The sparkle of the black sequin halter dress reminded her of a more fun version of herself, one she was determined to find once again. Feeling more upbeat, she placed the box by the door just as she heard a knock.

'Who is it?' she asked as she scrambled to find something to pull over her dress.

'Just me,' came James's voice.

Conscious that she was taking a while, she grabbed a cardigan off her bed before she opened the door.

'Wow… you look great. Sorry, is this a bad time?' he asked, his eyes darting nervously.

'Thanks… No, I was just looking for something to wear. I mean, not for today. For later. For the office Christmas party,' blabbered Annabel, trying to tug the dress down, conscious of the amount of her skin on show.

'It looks great,' replied James, regaining his composure.

'Thanks, but I'm not sure about it. It's a bit too…'

'Well, I think it looks great on you,' he said pausing. 'So, you decided to go? I thought you weren't too keen on it.'

'No, I wasn't. It's a long story. I just hope I won't regret it.'

'I'm sure it will be a good laugh,' said James. 'Anyway, I just came to bring this by. Ran into the postman downstairs and said I'd drop it off.'

'Thanks. God, I hope it's not another weird gift,' said Annabel, taking the parcel.

'Pardon?'

'It's another long story. Do you want to come in?'

'Sure. As long as I'm not disturbing.'

James took a seat on the sofa, Marley quickly taking up his place next to him whilst Annabel disappeared into the bedroom to get changed.

'Do you want a tea or a coffee?' Annabel asked, appearing from her room.

'A coffee would be nice. But are you sure I'm not in your way?'

'Positive. I have a couple of hours before I head into the city.'

'Doing anything nice?' enquired James.

'I need to find a dress for the party and I'm meeting my mum for lunch. We're going to the theatre later.'

'Sounds great,' said James.

'Yeah…'

'You don't sound too sure.'

'It's just, it's my mother. I mean she is nice and all, if you're not me.'

'So how come you've decided to meet her, then?'

Annabel proceeded to tell James about the Advent calendar and the tasks: how she ended up agreeing to spend Christmas with her family, how she'd said 'yes' to going along to the Christmas party, and now to spending more time with the strongest critic of her life, her mother.

'And you still have no idea who sent you the calendar?' asked James, taking a sip of his drink.

'I have my suspicions. It's got to be my mother. Who else would devise something so devious? She knows I couldn't just *not* do it.'

'It's possible. But maybe it wasn't her. Have you asked her about it?'

'No point. She would just deny it.'

'So you're just going to play along?'

'Well, I've started it now.'

'What was today's challenge?'

Annabel handed James the note.

'That's not too bad,' he said. 'And how is working with Sandra going?'

'You know. Ups and downs. More downs than ups at the minute. But I'm managing.'

Annabel started to open the parcel James brought along, half expecting it to be another anonymous delivery. The sender's details were clearly visible on the outside of the envelope and as she opened it, she realised it was the manuscript from Herold & Hains.

'She could have just given this to me on Monday,' she said as she placed it on the dining table. 'If I didn't know better, I'd think she does this on purpose.' The manuscript was adorned with colourful Post-it notes bearing Sandra's handwriting.

James glanced at the header on the first page. 'Is that the new project you're working on?' he asked.

'Yes, the one that's driving me mad at the moment. You remember my presentation, the one you recovered for the pitch? It was meant to be based on this book.'

'Meant to be?' asked James.

'I scrapped it last minute.'

'Was it that bad?'

'No. It's the opposite. It's really original, but it's a risky project to take on. I just had a great feeling about it. And I wish I'd stuck with it. If it wasn't for a comment Sandra made, I would have never changed my pitch. Anyway, I have no idea why she sent me a full new copy of it when I already had one.'

'It's great you still get to work on it.'

'Yes, but under Little Miss I-Know-Better's direction. She wants to completely rip the core premise away and turn it into a blockbuster and expects me to do all the work for her. It's ludicrous really.'

'So what are you going to do?'

'I don't know. I've tried to appeal to her better nature but not sure she has one. She said she'd think about it if I could find a way to make the original idea commercially appealing.

But she wasn't too enthusiastic about it. She'd rather I just got on with changing the whole thing. That's why I'd agreed to go along to the Christmas party. Well, that and the Advent calendar. I thought I might be able to convince her. But I'm starting to question my decision.'

Soon after James had left, Annabel made her way to one of the charity shops on her local high street, carrying the box of donations.

'Good morning. How can I help you?' said a cheery shop assistant with a beaming smile.

'I've brought some things to donate,' she replied.

'Great. Is it clothes, books or household items?'

'Just some clothes.'

'Let me take it from you.' He leant over the counter to take the box. As he put it down, he noticed Annabel looking at the bookshelf behind him.

'We've got some more over there if you fancy a browse,' he said, gesturing at the shelves on the other side of the shop.

From the outside the shop looked small, but once you stepped inside, it seemed to carry on for miles into the back. It seemed that you could find everything that anybody could have ever owned in there, as well as anything one could ever possibly need. The clothes rails were crammed full of mismatched items, shelves stacked with picture frames, soft toys and kitchenware, electrical gadgets, ornamental lamps, and boxes full of bric-a-brac. And of course, there was a seasonal section for all things festive.

Annabel was drawn to the rows of books at the far end. She spent a good half hour browsing through them and really had to restrain herself not to buy anything. Afterall, she was meant to give her possessions away, not acquire new ones.

When she finally got to the city, it was bustling with shoppers, with festive decorations everywhere, and Christmas music playing in the shops. Evelyn's train was due any minute and Annabel waited outside the station. She felt slightly nauseous as her thoughts turned to the afternoon ahead. She still hadn't told her mother about her break up and the anticipation of the level of disapproval to come was getting too much to bear. The large overhead sign confirmed that the train was on time, and it wasn't long before she started waiving at an approaching figure. Determined not to let the emotions get the better of her, she took a deep breath and walked towards her.

She could always spot her mother in any crowd. One thing she really admired her for was her impeccable dress sense. She always looked sophisticated and elegant without overdoing it.

'Hello, darling,' said Evelyn as she approached.

'Hi, Mum. Did you have a good journey?'

'A bit busy, but it was pleasant enough. Have you been waiting for long?'

'No, just got here about ten minutes ago.'

Evelyn had some Christmas shopping to finish off and Annabel was on a mission to find the perfect dress for the party, so after the pleasantries they set off in the direction of the crowds.

Her mother bought a couple of small gifts for Mrs Shepherd and Miss Lucas from church, and Annabel selected a few dresses ready to take to the changing room. The act of shopping served as a much-needed distraction. It gave them both something to do without having to think too much about the conversation. Annabel kept to topics they couldn't easily disagree on. She asked how everyone was back home and how Aunty Amelia was doing. She was keen to avoid any discussion about David or her work, especially the missed promotion. Restricting her words wasn't easy, but she had learnt through the years how to keep away from confrontation, and it mostly worked but it also fuelled a build up of unspoken pain.

She tried on the first two dresses, but the first one didn't leave much to the imagination and no matter how she wriggled, she couldn't quite find a comfortable position wearing the second one. *I bet Abi would look stunning in this dress*, she thought as she peeled it off her skin. Her hair looked even more frazzled than usual by the time she got out of the second dress.

Feeling increasingly hot, and with growing unease that she might not find anything appropriate to wear for the party, she moved to the third outfit, her enthusiasm dwindling quickly.

'So, how's David?' came Evelyn's voice from outside the cubicle.

Annabel could feel her heart racing as she caught her breath. 'He's fine,' she replied curtly, trying to compose herself. *You can't keep this from her forever, you know,* scolded her internal critic.

'Could you give me a hand?' she asked, steering the conversation away from dangerous ground. 'This zip is a bit tricky.'

Evelyn was happy to oblige, and with the zip pulled up Annabel turned around.

'What do you think?' she asked her mother.

Evelyn looked her up and down for a few moments before she said, 'It really suits you.'

Annabel turned to look in the mirror and for once she had to agree with her mother. She loved the colour, the style, and everything about it. The dress was perfect in every way. Satisfied that she had found what she was looking for, she headed to the checkout.

'Glad that's sorted. I don't think I could have kept looking for much longer,' said Annabel as they left the shop. 'I'm getting a bit hungry.'

'I wouldn't mind some lunch either,' said Evelyn.

Annabel knew her mother wasn't a fan of exotic cuisines especially after the unfortunate incident a couple of years ago when her chicken korma was mixed up with someone's vindaloo. Her palate was more accustomed to European-style food, so they settled on Browns. Annabel sunk into the chair as they took their place at the table.

'I still don't see the appeal of doing this on a regular basis. It's only been a couple of hours and I feel shattered,' she said.

Despite the Christmas crowds the staff was efficient as ever and their food arrived promptly.

'I had a great time today,' said Evelyn. 'It's been lovely to spend some time with you. I don't get to see you that often anymore.'

Annabel hoped her mother would spare her one of her usual speeches about why she didn't stay in Masham.

'Yes, it's been nice today,' Annabel said, her emotions balancing on a tightrope.

'I'm so glad you'll join us this year for Christmas,' said Evelyn. 'Has David not changed his mind about joining us?'

'No, I'll be coming up on my own,' replied Annabel with growing unease. The pressure inside her chest was getting more and more uncomfortable and after her earlier emotional wobble in the morning, she couldn't contain her inner turmoil anymore. 'We broke up,' she said finally.

'When?' asked Evelyn.

'A couple of weeks ago.'

'Oh, what a shame. He seemed like a nice man. What brought this on?'

Annabel stayed silent. She knew it was only a matter of time before her career choice was scrutinised and her mother decimated her self-worth once again.

'Was there another woman?' asked Evelyn.

'No. There was nothing like that,' said Annabel, hesitating for a moment. 'He wanted me to stop pursuing the editor role and he thought I would step it down when I was turned down for the promotion.'

'Well, that's not that unreasonable,' said Evelyn.

'Thanks, Mum.'

'I'm just being honest. Maybe it's time to rethink this career path of yours.'

'Here we go again. I'm sorry if I'm letting you down, Mum,' she said, her heart pounding at the thought of what was to come.

'Letting me down? You're not letting me down. I just hoped you'd be happy by now. Settle down, have your own family.'

'Maybe my career makes me happy.'

'That's not the same.'

'It's like there's only one way that I can be happy in your eyes. You've never really considered what I want,' pleaded Annabel, fighting back the tears.

'I've always felt like I let you down, you know. Like I could never do as well as Abi did. Like what I did was never enough,' she continued as tears started to roll down her cheeks. 'I bet that's why you sent me that Advent box.'

'What Advent box?' asked Evelyn, looking confused. 'I have no idea what you're talking about, darling. But it was never a competition. I've always loved you both the same. And you haven't let me down. I'm so proud that you are standing on your own two feet and have the conviction to follow your dreams. I'm just worried. I want the best for both of you and sometimes I have a hard time keeping my feelings to myself. And maybe I don't find the best way to express them. You always had a way with words… It's not my forte.'

Annabel went quiet, her stream of tears ebbing. She was expecting a different reaction. It wasn't often her mother complimented her and even rarer that she admitted to her own flaws. For a second, she didn't know how to react. She wanted to savour the moment and frame it in her mind. It was like a rare bird. If you scared it away, you might never see it again.

'I'm sorry you and David broke up. And not because I see having a family as the only way to happiness, but because I don't want you to be unhappy. And I feel awful that you didn't feel you could confide in me and had to carry this all on your own, thinking I might disapprove.'

'Lucy kind of held the fort. And I'm fine. But it's nice to know you care.'

'Of course, I do,' said Evelyn, hugging her daughter.

'So, you didn't send me the Advent calendar?' asked Annabel, withdrawing from her mother's embrace.

'No. I haven't bought those in years. Not since you were kids. Your dad always nags me to get one, but with his blood sugar I stay away from them. Did someone send you one in my name?'

'No, it just arrived one day without a sender. I thought it was you. It's probably just a mistake,' said Annabel. She was so sure her mother was behind the gift, but now she had no idea who could have been the one who'd sent it.

'Any coffee or tea?' asked the waiter, appearing next to their table.

Annabel glanced at her watch. 'No, thank you. Just the bill. We'd better get going if we don't want to miss the show.'

Hurrying across the streets, they arrived at the theatre just before the last call. The performance was everything she remembered it to be. The vintage toys, the giant tree, the dancers bringing the magic of Christmas to life. Captivated by the music, she embraced the comfort of nostalgia, reliving a fond childhood memory. When the curtains fell with the last bow, it was a fitting end to a surprisingly pleasant day.

Chapter 5

After finding out that her mother wasn't behind the calendar, Annabel was even more baffled as to who could have sent her this unusual gift. Thinking back to the tasks earlier in the week, she was sure David wouldn't have picked most of these. He thought she spent enough time already at work and burying her head in books, so he wouldn't have encouraged her to do more of that. Whoever the mysterious sender was, she couldn't be sure if they were friend or foe. Trying to waft away the unwelcome thoughts, she planned to take a day of well-earned rest after a busy week. She was going to catch up on her reading for next week's book club and enjoy a quiet day in. That was her plan, until she opened the next window on her Advent calendar.

Do a random act of kindness

Set on finding a way to complete the task without having to leave her flat that day, she was full of ideas about how she could do something positive. *I could give to a charity or start to fundraise for a good cause. I could send some flowers and a nice card or just a nice message to someone random, or buy a gift for one of the local Christmas toy drives*, she thought. Annabel wasn't short on ideas. So, she sat back contently sipping her morning cup of coffee, confident that she had a lot of options to choose from.

Her plans were soon foiled when she opened the fridge. She was meant to do a food shop on Friday on her way home from work, but she forgot after getting back late and being out most of the day on Saturday. Now she was looking at a near-empty fridge.

There'll be something in the freezer. She usually had some emergency rations in there but remembered eating the last pizza the day before. *I could order some food,* she thought. *But then I'd have to do the shopping on Monday, and I've got a busy day planned.* Reluctantly she accepted that she'd have to venture out.

Going out was one thing, but having to get out of her loungewear and into something far less comfortable was another. The nearest shop was only a five-minute walk away and as she scrutinised her outfit, she contemplated whether she could get away with not changing and just wearing a long winter coat over it. Leggings might be back in fashion, but Annabel never liked the thought of her bottom being on show like that and her t-shirt certainly didn't help with this. It was one of the only mementoes she kept from a previous relationship and not for sentimental reasons. She simply liked it. It had been in the wash many times and had faded and stretched over the years; but not enough to pass the bottom-covering test. *The long coat should solve the problem.*

She got ready to leave and as she opened her front door, she realised she'd left her phone on the table. She quickly grabbed it, but with the door still half open, Marley decided to try his luck and escape. By the time Annabel noticed what he was up to, it was too late to stop him. Closing the door behind her, she dashed after him. He headed down the corridor and disappeared a couple of doors down. Annabel had just managed to work out where he went when the door closed in front of her. After knocking and waiting for a reply, she was surprised when she saw a familiar face emerge as the door re-opened.

'Mr Adler! Hi. I'm really sorry to bother you but I think my cat might have snuck into your flat just now.'

The elderly man seemed puzzled by her proposition and didn't answer for a second.

'He doesn't usually do this,' continued Annabel, slightly raising her voice as she remembered about his hearing.

'I don't think I've seen him come in, but come and have a look. He might be hiding somewhere,' said Mr Adler with a slight cheek in his voice.

Annabel followed him into the flat, closing the door behind her. She noticed a couple of photos on the dresser in the hallway as she walked past, and a few more as they entered the living room. No frills or unnecessary clutter anywhere. Just reserved, functional minimalism.

'There he is,' said Annabel, still shouting. Marley was sat proudly on a comfortable-looking armchair close to the window.

'I'm so sorry, Mr Adler. I'm not sure what's got into him. He's never run off like that before.'

'I see you have good taste, old fella. That's also my favourite spot.'

'That's very naughty, Marley. We'll get out of your way, Mr Adler. I'm really sorry to have bothered you like this.'

'It was no bother at all. It's nice to have visitors, even if it's only for a short while. Would you like to stay for a cup of tea?'

'Erm... that's very kind of you, but we don't want to impose.'

'You're not imposing, And I've just got some biscuits from the shop. All butter, if you like that sort.'

'All right. A cup of tea and a biscuit would be nice.'

Annabel sat down on the sofa still in her coat, clutching Marley. As she looked around the room, she noticed how large it seemed compared to her own. A two-seater sofa dominated the room and there weren't many other items apart from the armchair by the window, a small coffee table and a cabinet with a record player by the door.

Looking around, Annabel couldn't help but notice the absence of a television. She didn't own one herself and had been asked many times how she could live without one. 'I don't have time,' was her excuse most of the time, but if she was completely honest, she preferred to imagine the worlds she read about rather than have them created for her.

Aside from the imposing grandfather clock, the magnolia walls were only covered by a few photographs and a couple of framed military medals. Minutes later, Mr Adler returned from the kitchen with two cups of tea and a plateful of shortbread on a tray.

'Thank you,' said Annabel.

'You don't have to shout, you know. I can hear perfectly well with these in. I just like to have the option to turn the volume down and pretend I can't hear when I don't want to enter a conversation. They've been a godsend at times. Especially when Mrs Humphries is around with those noisy twins.'

Annabel was surprised by the revelation but found it rather amusing. She always thought that Mr Adler was just a bit grumpy, but she was beginning to warm to him.

It was warm in the flat and Annabel was getting increasingly uncomfortable. *Older people seem to like to keep their place hot*, she thought, and soon wearing her coat was getting unbearable. But the thought of sitting there in a worn t-shirt and leggings made her even more uncomfortable; especially as Mr Adler was dressed so impeccably. When she came to think of it, it wasn't often she had seen anyone in her grandmother's generation looking shabby. They always seemed to be dressed for an occasion, even if that occasion was going to the shop. In contrast to the faded letters that ran across the front of her t-shirt, reading "Frankie says relax", she was anything but relaxed but she decided to compromise on undoing her coat zip.

'How long have you lived here for?' she asked.

'It'll be fifteen years in April. We moved here after Dotty decided the house was getting a bit much to look after. So, we downsized. She passed away eight years ago. Cancer.'

'I'm sorry to hear that. Losing her must have been hard.' Annabel felt a pang of guilt that she didn't even know his name until a couple of days ago.

'It hasn't always been easy. My son, Charlie wanted me to move to Australia with them. He's concerned that I'm here by myself. But I like it here.'

'Is that him?' asked Annabel, gesturing at a photo on the wall.

'Yes. That's Ruth, my daughter-in-law, and my granddaughters Jade and Hayley.'

'You've got a lovely family. It must be hard, them being so far away.'

'I do miss them, but we speak often. They even got me one of those mobile gadgets to call on. I'm not keen on those things, but it's nice to see their faces when we talk. How about you? Do you have family nearby?'

'Not in London. My parents and my little sister live up north. Well, I say little sister, but she turned thirty-two this year.'

'Some things never change,' said Mr Adler. 'I still refer to Margot as my little sister and she's nearing eighty.'

Annabel smiled, memories filtering in through her mind.

'Are you two close?' asked Mr Adler.

'Me and my sister? We used to be. We were inseparable when we were younger. Little rascals, Mum used to call us. We were always on the go, climbing trees and creating our own magical worlds, like children do, I suppose. Mum was forever concerned about us falling off something.' Annabel smiled, her mother's words echoing in her mind. *I told you not to climb on that tree again.* 'I moved to London to start university and Abi stayed up north. She studied to become a doctor. She's taking over her local GP practice and I've been focused on work too. We just haven't seen each other that much in the last few years. But I know it's not as far as Australia.'

'No, I suppose it's not. But even a few hundred miles can be a bit tricky, can't it?' asked Mr Adler, with all-knowing eyes.

'Are your family visiting for Christmas?' asked Annabel.

'Yes, they're arriving in a couple of weeks.'

'I'm sure that'll be lovely.'

Mr Adler nodded as he looked around. 'I haven't really bothered with decorations since Dotty passed,' he said, gesturing at the bare walls. 'She was good at that sort of thing. Making things look nice.'

Annabel hadn't noticed the lack of Christmas décor in the room before. But once he mentioned it, it was painfully obvious. They'd been chatting for a while when Marley started to get a bit restless, so Annabel thought they should get going. She thanked Mr Adler for the tea and biscuits and made her excuses to leave. Taking Marley back to her own place, a thought occurred to her. She'd leave the flat after all, but first she had to get changed.

Half an hour later she was on her way back to the charity shop. She remembered the large box full of Christmas decorations they had next to the bookshelves. Elbow deep, she rummaged through the box and picked out a handful of white and silver baubles, a box of tinsel, and she even found some fairy lights on the electrical appliances shelf.

'I see you're back,' the shop assistant greeted her. 'These baubles are gorgeous,' he said, scanning them and placing them in a bag.

'They're lovely. You don't sell Christmas trees, by any chance?' she asked.

'We had an artificial one last week, but we've sold that, I'm afraid. They have some cute little ones in the supermarket a few doors down, though.'

'I'll check that out. Thank you.'

Armed with the decorations, she headed to the shop to pick up a few things for herself and to find a tree. She was slightly concerned that her new acquaintance might find the whole thing intrusive. *What's the worst thing that could happen?* He'd think she was a busybody and she'd have two trees in her flat. *Not ideal*, she thought, but she was willing to take her chances.

It wasn't long before she had a plan and a box full of supplies. For the second time that day she found herself in front of number twenty-nine.

Mr Adler seemed surprised to see Annabel again when he opened the door.

'Twice in one day. To what do I owe this pleasure? Have you forgotten something?'

'No, I haven't. You were so welcoming earlier, and I wanted to do something nice in return. Of course, you're free to say no, but I thought I could bring some of the festivities to your place.' She lifted the Christmas tree.

'I completely understand if you don't want me butting in; I just thought you might like it.'

The elderly man looked at Annabel and then the tree. The silence made her nervous. 'It sounds lovely,' he said finally. 'I'd really like that.'

Annabel sighed out in relief. 'Great. I promise I'll clear it away after Christmas as well. Don't worry about being left with the remnants.'

Mr Adler pointed out where the tree could go: in the perfect position so he could see it when sitting in his chair. Annabel turned the tree around to show off its best side and made a start on unpacking the decorations.

'What kind of music do you listen to?' she asked, gesturing at the record player.

'Opera, mostly. Me and Dotty often went to the theatre on a Friday night. Puccini's *La bohème* was one of her favourites. We must have seen it three times at least.'

'How lovely. I don't think I've ever seen it,' said Annabel.

'You might have heard the music before,' he said. 'Would you like to have a listen?'

'I don't want to trouble you if you'd rather not.'

'It's no trouble. I haven't listened to it in a while.'

He walked over to the cabinet and pulled a record out of its sleeve, placing it on the turntable. The soft crackle of the record was soon followed by the playful entrance of the orchestra and beautiful baritone and tenor voices. Annabel enjoyed the music and had been busy in the living room wrapping fairy lights around the tree while Mr Adler disappeared into the bedroom.

'The music is beautiful. I only wish I could understand what they're singing,' she said as he returned with a small box in his hand and placed it on the coffee table.

'They're singing about love and the difficulties of life. The opening scene is set on Christmas Eve,' said Mr Adler as he sat down on the sofa. He sat there for a while listening to the record before he lifted the box's lid. 'I didn't keep many of these, but they were Dotty's favourite. She put them up on the tree every year.'

Annabel turned to him to take a look. The box was full of etched glass baubles. All different shapes, wrapped in white tissue paper.

'They're beautiful.' She took one of them out and delicately placed it in the middle of the tree. 'What do you think about it there?' she asked.

Mr Adler's steel blue eyes misted over as he looked at the bauble gently twirling. 'It looks perfect. Dotty would have loved it.'

'I think we are ready for the light switch on.' *I should've checked first that the lights work. It's too late now, anyway.* Annabel crossed her fingers, flicked the switch by the plug and hoped that they would come on.

To both of their delights, the lights illuminated the tree and with it the room; the baubles shimmered in their glow. They stood there for a while mesmerised by the sight, when Mr Adler broke their silence. 'Would you like a mince pie?'

He could see that Annabel was about to make a polite excuse and before she could reply he went on, 'I think you've earnt it after all this hard work and it would be nice to chat a bit longer.'

'A mince pie sounds lovely,' said Annabel with a smile.

***

Annabel was filled with festive cheer after a pleasant weekend. Work-life balance had started to become more of a reality, and she was feeling better than she had done in years. The tasks didn't faze her as much as they did at the beginning. She looked forward to doing something different each day and was excited to see what the little window of number ten had in store for her.

Reconnect with someone you've lost touch with

Reading the task felt jarring after her pleasant start to the day. As much as Annabel wanted to deny it, she was painfully aware of the number of relationships she had lost over the years and her thoughts went straight to her latest fail with David. She was devastated when he ended things between them, and she was acutely aware that the main reason was down to her. Over the last few weeks, she'd thought of texting him many times, but as the days went by, she thought maybe it was for the better that she didn't.

Aside from David, many other people in her life had come and gone. Friendships from school and university, colleagues from work. Relationships that didn't work out for one reason or another. She had heard and used the phrase many times before: 'It's not you, it's me'. Was it true or was it just the easy way out?

Only a handful of connections – like her friendship with Lucy – really stood the test of time. She didn't think much of it before. She thought losing touch with people over time was just a way of life. Paths crossed and then diverged. Nothing unusual. But this task made her think. Were there relationships she'd given up on too easily or was she ever too proud to make the first move? Probably.

She needed time to think and figure this one out.

Annabel found herself being surprisingly friendly with Sandra when she got to work.

'How was the food on Friday?' she asked as she approached Sandra's desk.

Sandra hesitated slightly before she answered. 'The food? Oh, it was amazing! Better than I remembered from last time. We had a few drinks; probably more than we should have done. But it was good fun,' she said.

'Sounds great. Sorry I couldn't join you. Maybe next time.'

'Definitely. Sorry, but I've got to dash off. I still have some stuff to sort out with Thomas before the meeting.'

They seem to be talking a lot recently. I suppose it must be about her new role, thought Annabel.

'You two seem to be getting on like a house on fire,' remarked Liv as her and Annabel headed to the Monday morning meeting.

'Just being polite, Liv. But somehow, I agreed to come to the Christmas party on Friday.'

'Never! How did that happen? I thought you couldn't think of many things worse to do.'

'That's not quite what I said, but it's close,' admitted Annabel. 'Anyway, I'm trying to keep an open mind.'

'Great. You can sit next to me and Ben.'

'You'll have to speak to Sandra about that. She's organised the seating plan and I'm supposed to be sitting next to her… Couldn't really say no.'

'You really are a much better person than I am, Annabel. I don't think I could be so pally with her if they gave my job to her.'

'There's no point dwelling on that, Liv. They clearly thought she'd do a better job than me. She got it fair and square. Besides, I'm trying to get her to change her mind about this new project direction. She said if I can show her the original plan is commercially viable, she might consider sticking with it.'

'Ha, good luck with that.'

As the day went on, Annabel didn't have much time to think about her challenge. But on her way home her mind kept going back to the same place, to the same person again and again. Closing that door of her life wasn't a pain-free process and she wasn't sure she was ready to open it again, so she scanned her past in search of other failed relations.

She reminisced about her school days back in Masham. The long summers and times she spent with her Nana Margaret in Cornwall, hiding in the tall grass at the back of the house. A lot of fond memories. She thought of her university days when she first moved to London and her first rented apartment in the city. Being terrified and excited all at the same time. She remembered colleagues from her first day at Herold & Hains and wondered where they were today.

But her mind drew her back to the same place as she remembered coming across a box over the weekend whilst looking for things to donate. Surrendering to the thought, she headed to her bedroom to retrieve it. She sat down on the couch and took the lid off. A few smaller boxes were inside and a couple of photo albums. She opened one of them. They were from her final year at uni. Her hair was much shorter and ironed straight. She was wearing a crop top, skinny jeans and her old leather jacket. She wondered if she could pull off a look like that again. The photo was taken outside the Windsor Building. The girl sitting next to her had long brown hair. She wore a red jumper, dark blue jeans, and a pair of brown leather boots. Becca.

She took the photo out of the album and turned it around but there was nothing written on the back. Becca and Annabel had run the student newspaper together and spent most of their time in each other's company for five years. After they graduated, Becca got a job at a London magazine and Annabel started working at Herold & Hains.

Still staring at the photo, Annabel's thoughts turned to the person behind the camera that day. She'd been close to Adam from early on. Like Annabel, he was a northerner. He was charismatic and Annabel liked his persistence.

They started dating in their second year and just after graduating Adam proposed. He wanted to move back up north and settle down, but Annabel's ambitions were set on a different path. She was intent on making it as an editor in London. It soon became apparent that they couldn't make things work and Adam moved back up north. Annabel was devastated, but her new job at Herold & Hains gave her something to focus on.

At first, she met up with Becca quite regularly, but soon their encounters got less and less frequent, until after about a year and a half of quiet Becca had arranged for them to meet out of the blue.

Thinking back, Annabel felt excited to see her friend again, but Becca was visibly nervous as soon as Annabel walked through the door. And the cause of her anxiousness soon became apparent when Becca confessed that her and Adam had been back in touch.

'He rang up about a job we advertised, and we started chatting. We met up and… things just happened. We never intended for this to become anything. It was just two old friends catching up.'

Annabel still remembered how she sat motionless; her frame frozen into a permanent shape.

'I wasn't even sure if things were going anywhere, and I didn't want to upset you, so I didn't say anything,' said Becca. 'But last week things had changed.' The image of Becca nervously fidgeting with her hands was etched into Annabel's memory. 'Adam proposed,' Becca said finally. 'I feel awful that

I haven't said anything to you until now. I just didn't know how to bring it up and I didn't want to cause any pain,' said Becca.

Annabel's stomach was in knots and her mouth went dry. 'Wow… that's a surprise. Adam came back to London?' Annabel managed to ask.

'Things just didn't work out for him up north, so he decided to come back,' Becca said nervously.

'He never said,' mumbled Annabel, staring in front of her.

'I don't think he told anyone from the old crew… I'm so sorry. I should have said something earlier.'

'Don't be. We broke up a long time ago and it's none of my business who he dates,' replied Annabel, trying to sound unaffected.

'So, you're okay with this?' asked Becca.

'Of course,' said Annabel, contorting her face into a smile. 'I'm happy for you both.'

Relieved, Becca embraced her friend. 'I'm so glad you're not mad. Adam is going to be relieved too.'

There was a pregnant pause between them before Annabel spoke again. 'So, when's the big day?' she asked.

'In June.'

Annabel thought she was through the worst of Becca's shock revelation, until Becca asked her to be her bridesmaid.

'I totally get it if that's too much, but it would mean the world to me… and to Adam,' said Becca. 'You don't have to tell me now, but just have a think about it.'

It took a couple of days for Annabel to process the news, but eventually she decided that things between her Adam were over a long time ago and that she wanted to be there for her friends. So, she accepted the invite.

Things were going well but with work getting busier she missed a couple of the dress fittings. She also had to cancel going to Becca's hen do because of a deadline at work. When Annabel mentioned a book fair on the same weekend as the wedding, Becca got upset and told her that if she couldn't be on board, then maybe she shouldn't come to the wedding at all.

Annabel told her it wasn't anything to do with them, it was just work and tried to patch things up, but Becca had made up her mind.

Annabel didn't want to cause any more upset, especially on Becca's big day, so she decided it was best if she stayed away. As the weeks went by it seemed increasingly more difficult to pick up the phone. She tried to push the guilt to a far corner of her mind, but she often wondered how Becca might be doing.

Returning from her memories to the present moment, Annabel looked Becca up on social media. True to her word, Becca hadn't budged on her insistence on keeping her surname after the wedding, so she wasn't too difficult to find.

She hesitated for a moment wondering what to write. How do you start a message to someone you haven't spoken to for years? In the end, she settled on ***Hi***.

Annabel didn't expect a response, and definitely not straight away. So, when she heard a ping, she felt a sudden pang of anxiety. But her angst soon dissipated as they got off to a surprisingly good start.

Are you still on the same number? asked Becca.

Just as Annabel sent the reply, her phone rang. Her heart started beating faster and after a split second of hesitation, she answered the call. Annabel expected it to feel strange hearing Becca's voice after so many years, but it wasn't one bit. It felt like they'd only spoken last week and soon she felt comfortable in their conversation.

'How's Adam doing?' asked Annabel after some time.

'I'm not quite sure. We decided to go our separate ways about two years ago. Haven't spoken to him since.'

'I'm so sorry. I didn't know,' said Annabel.

'Don't be. He turned into his dad, the lying bastard.'

'Oh my God, that's horrible.'

'I should have seen the signs. They were so obvious when I look back.'

'It must have been difficult for you.'

'It was for a while, but I'm in a much better place now. I'm with someone else and things are going really well. We got engaged three months ago.'

'Congratulations. I'm so happy for you. I still feel awful about what happened back then. I should have been there for you. I was so focused on my career and everything else seemed to fade into the background. I'm sorry.'

'It's me who should apologise. I still feel awful for putting you in that position. I shouldn't have expected you to be on board with all that.'

'Thanks for saying that,' said Annabel.

'I've really missed our chats, you know,' said Becca.

'Ditto.'

'It'd be nice to meet up sometime when you're free.'

'I'd love that.'

'I'm in the city most days so just let me know when you are available after work, and we can meet up somewhere.'

They agreed a date, time and place before she hung up the phone.

As she laid in bed that night Annabel quietly contemplated the difficult conversations she'd had over the past couple of weeks. As much as she dreaded them at first, the catharsis of starting to untangle years of built-up guilt and resentment had been liberating.

Chapter 6

Annabel's day was off to a good start. She took a last-minute holiday and was enjoying her lie in. As her outlook on life progressively improved each day, Annabel felt she could take on any challenge that was thrown at her; or at least face it with a positive attitude. Feeling a sense of excitement, she opened window number eleven on the calendar.

Commit to a challenge you've always wanted to do

'Challenge.' She savoured the word.

Annabel had often seen people doing challenges on social media. Climbing mountains, cycling the length and breadth of the country, taking part in endurance events and even skydiving to raise money for a good cause. She wasn't sure either of these things were the kind of challenge she was looking for. She was terrified of heights and the last time she sat on a bike was when she was fifteen.

When she thought about it, though, there was one thing she always aspired to do but the challenge had seemed too great, and life somehow got in the way. This was her chance to commit and make it a reality.

She was set on what she wanted to do but the 'where' was still a question. After browsing on the internet for an hour or so she found the perfect place. The process was relatively straight forward, and it wasn't long before she had signed up to run at the Loch Ness Marathon next year. The London event might have been more of an obvious choice given her location, but she wanted to run a marathon somewhere a bit different. The legend of Loch Ness had always fascinated her as a child and the route promised to be truly breath-taking. Plus, the race was in October, which gave her plenty of time to prepare. Having the aspiration was one thing, but she always managed to convince herself that she was far too busy to fit training in. Now she had no excuses. The event might have been months away, but she knew it that preparing for it took a lot of effort, planning and dedication.

The weather looked pleasant enough outside for a winter's day even if it was a little cold. The faint winter sunshine was all the encouragement she needed. She made her way to her wardrobe and pulled out a large box. Taking the lid off, she trawled through the contents.

I must remember not to buy any more black shoes next time I'm in the shop, she thought, putting aside the third pair.

'Finally,' she exclaimed, holding up one turquoise running shoe. 'I just need the other one,' she continued, flinging a couple of shoes out of the way. 'There it is.'

She started to rummage through another drawer. 'I'm sure I put it in here somewhere,' she mumbled. The pile on the floor grew rapidly before she emerged with a smart watch in her hand. 'I knew it was here.'

Abi bought her the gadget a while back and as much as it was a thoughtful gift, Annabel often forgot to charge it. She wore it to her last exercise class a week or so ago, but the battery had gone flat since, so she put it on to charge before completing a thorough session of stretching and devouring an energy bar. 'Twenty percent. This will do,' she said, strapping the watch on her wrist, ready to go. Armed with an upbeat playlist, she headed to the local park.

As she set off, she was conscious of not wanting to overdo it. *A mile or so would do for a first run*, just to see how she did with that. The first few hundred meters were easy enough and soon she got into a comfortable rhythm. Maybe it was the cold or the time of day, but there weren't many other people around, so she had most of the path to herself.

Closing in on the first mile, she had to dig deep. The first run was proving to be harder than she envisaged it to be. Just as she was about to stop, *Eye Of The Tiger* came on. The track was just the encouragement she needed to carry on.

Back in the zone, her mind was sharp once more. She was determined to complete at least another half mile. All her attention was focused on keeping her breathing even. The world around her almost faded out of vision, so much so that she didn't see the man running on the path across hers until it was too late.

She crashed into him, the music still loud in her ear.

She took her earphones out.

'What the…,' said the man stunned.

'I'm so sorry. I don't know where my mind was. I didn't see you there. Are you all right?' she asked.

When she bent down to help him up, she realised who she had knocked over. 'James! Oh my God, I'm so sorry. Are you all right?'

'Oh, it's you,' he said, sounding a bit less irritated. 'I'm okay. Just a bit of dirt and a few scrapes. Nothing that some water won't clean off.'

He got up quickly, dusting himself off.

'I didn't know you ran,' he said.

'I didn't. I mean, I haven't for a long time but decided to start back up again.'

'The Advent calendar?' he asked.

'Yeah.' Smiled Annabel.

'It's certainly a nice day for a run. But if I can give you a bit of advice, you might want to brush up on the running rules before you go out again.'

'Rules? I know I haven't been running for a while, but I didn't know there were rules now.'

'Oh, yes. And rule number one is watch where you're going.'

Annabel laughed. 'Thanks, I'll keep that in mind for next time. I think I'm finished for the day anyway. Just over a mile will do me for a first run.'

'Yeah, you don't want to overdo it. How come you're not at work at this time anyway?'

'On holiday today. Still had a few days to use before Christmas.'

'Lucky you. I've got some work to do later but I'm going to head to the café down the road if you fancy joining me. They do a great pumpkin spice latte. It's a real treat after a run.'

'I'm not sure I've earned a treat, but it sounds great,' said Annabel, checking the time.

'Nice watch.'

'Thanks. My sister got it for me, but I haven't used it much to be honest.'

'It's got some cool features on it.'

'Really? I know it tells the time and shows me how fast my heart beats, but that's about as far as I've got with it.'

'There's a bit more to it.' Smiled James. 'I can set a couple of things up on it if you like and show you how it works. It could be useful for your runs.'

'Sure,' replied Annabel, handing him the watch.

'So how did your afternoon go with your mum the other day?' he asked.

'Better than expected, actually. I mean it's not like there weren't fireworks, but I think we might have had a breakthrough. Or maybe *I* might have had a breakthrough. But I don't want to jinx it. We have some way to go yet.'

'That's great. So have you found out if she sent you the calendar?'

'She was adamant she didn't, which was a disappointment. I could have sworn she was behind it.'

'So still no idea who sent it?'

'No, and I don't know if I'll ever find out,' she said as they headed out of the park.

By the time she got back to her flat it was nearly lunchtime. After a quick shower and some food, she made plans for the rest of the day. With half a day gone already, she still had a few errands to run before heading over to visit Mr Adler. Although she'd bought a couple of Christmas presents already and had some ideas for most of the others, she still had to figure what to buy for her sister.

After her afternoon at Mr Adler's place the other day, memories of her and Abi's childhood returned to her mind. Annabel remembered the photo albums in the box from the other day. She was flicking through the pictures when she came across one with the two of them grinning at the camera, their arms around each other's shoulders. Abi looked rather proud of the gaping hole where her two bottom teeth should have been. They must have been about eight and six, judging by the photo.

She recognised the matching pendants they wore: the silver suns holding a sparkling crystal in their centre. Their birthstones. Abi's was a moonstone and hers a beautiful green peridot. They were a Christmas gift from their grandmother. Annabel still had hers in a box but remembered the time when they came back from one of their summer adventures and Abi couldn't find hers. They returned the next day to look for it but couldn't find it anywhere. Abi was devastated. Their mother wasn't happy either, but it was her sister's sad face that really stuck with Annabel.

The photo gave her an idea. She grabbed her laptop and scrolled through a number of websites without luck before coming across a local shop's webpage. She jotted down the address. Glancing at the clock, she realised she still had time before her visit to Mr Adler.

Heading down the road a couple of streets away, Annabel walked past a newsagent and a small DIY shop before reaching a café at the end of the street. *I'm sure it was supposed to be here*, she thought before taking the note out of her pocket to check the address again. *Maybe they've moved*, she thought. The address was 10a Town Street.

She walked back, and found number 10 and number 12, but no 10a. Looking around for a sign, she noticed a narrow alleyway right next to number 10.

That's strange, she thought. She didn't remember the ginnel being there before, but thought she must have missed it when she walked past. Looking for a sign, she spotted a weathered board mounted to the brickwork, with faded letters only just visible:

Arlena's Box of Jewels.

The condition of the sign made her question whether the shop would still be there, but she headed down the path anyway, hoping to find out. The alley's cobblestones led to a small courtyard surrounded by four whitewashed brick walls, one with two large windows and a canary-yellow door with a large glass pane.

There wasn't anybody around, but Annabel saw the 'open' sign behind the glass and decided to go in. As she pushed the door open, the chimes above jingled softly. She closed the door behind her before looking around.

The shop seemed void of life but crammed with possessions. The towering pieces of mahogany furniture made the place feel small and dark, lit only by the sparkle of shiny items on display all around. A large silver gramophone horn was one of the most imposing items in the room.

A deep woody scent lingered around as Annabel made her way to the counter. The shop was quiet with only some faint piano music coming from the back. She stood there for a while admiring the pieces of jewellery behind the glass. Some ornate, some simple pieces, but each one was unique.

Finally, a woman appeared from the back. 'I'm sorry, I didn't hear you come in,' she said, pushing her glasses up the bridge of her nose.

'Don't worry, I wasn't waiting long. I've been admiring these pieces in the cabinet. They're beautiful.'

'Thank you. Is there something specific you're looking for or are you just browsing?' the woman asked.

'I'm after something quite specific, actually. I was wondering if you'd be able to create another one of these,' said Annabel, producing the pendant from her pocket.

'It was a gift from my grandmother. Me and my sister had identical ones, but hers went missing some time ago. I know it meant a lot to her and I've looked at replacing it, but I could never find one quite like it. Hers had a moonstone in the middle.'

The woman picked up the pendant and inspected it.

'I don't usually do replicas. I like things to be individual. Unique,' she said. 'Besides, the replica wouldn't be the same either. But I can see the sentimental attachment and I think I could make one that would look fairly close to the original.'

'It would mean a lot,' said Annabel.

'All right. When would you want it to be ready?' she asked. 'It shouldn't take long, but I'll need at least a week or so.'

'That would be perfect. As long as it's before Christmas it's fine,' said Annabel.

After settling on the price, the woman produced a small handwritten ticket. 'Come back on the 23rd. It'll be ready for then.'

Bitter cold winter darkness had fallen by the time Annabel stepped out of Arlena's shop. On the way back, she stopped at the supermarket to pick up some biscuits before heading over to see Mr Adler.

***

Annabel was getting ready for work. Feeling recharged after her day off and excited about seeing Becca later, she looked forward to the day ahead. She was glad she and Becca had got the initial awkwardness out of the way and hoped that they could be part of each other's lives once again.

In her excitement she almost forgot about her Advent calendar. With one shoe on, she hopped back from the hall and opened the window of number twelve. She grabbed the scroll, eagerly unrolling it as she made her way back down the hallway.

24 Windows

Surprise someone

As much as Annabel loved adventure and unpredictability when it came to stories, she wasn't a fan of surprises in everyday life. She'd have loved to be someone who could be swept off on a plane to a mystery destination and enjoy every minute of it, but in reality, that was one of her worst nightmares.

Surprises often seemed an inconvenience to her and no matter how well-meaning they were, they often turned out to be a disaster. Like the surprise party she had on her thirtieth birthday when all she wanted to do was to be alone and mourn the end of her twenties. The two Ps – planning and predictability – were suited to her much better. Despite her personal feelings about surprises, she was determined to complete the task. Besides, *other people might really like surprises*, she thought. Like getting Mr Adler a Christmas tree and decorations. *That was a gamble but thankfully it turned out to be a great success*.

As her day went on, she thought about what the people near and dear to her liked. She knew Liv loved French patisserie and surprising her with a box of her favourite treats might sound like a great idea, *but what if she's on a health kick?* She might absolutely hate it. Annabel had to think carefully if she was to get this right.

After some deliberation, she settled on an idea. Checking the time, she reached for her phone. It rang for a while and Annabel was just about to hang up when Abi answered.

'Hi, Annabel. What a lovely surprise.'

'I hope it's not a bad time?'

'No, I was just finishing my lunch.'

Despite not speaking often, Annabel knew her sister always took her lunch at the same time every day. Even with the clinic being busy she knew how particular Abi was about her routine.

'Thought so. I was calling to see if next Wednesday would be good for the dress fitting. Mum said you were busy and didn't want to leave things to the last minute, so I thought we could sort it then.'

'Let me check if I can get cover for that day. What time?'

'Don't know. Maybe around 11?'

'That might work, but I'll text you later. Hang on a sec, someone is calling on the other line.

'Don't worry, just let me know about next week,' said Annabel.

As she hung up the phone, Annabel was pleased. It seemed that the surprise was well-received, and her task for the day was complete.

Annabel left work on time and arrived early at the restaurant. The waiter showed her to a table where Becca was seated already. When she reached her friend, there was no hesitation by either of them as they greeted one another with a hug. Their friendship had a strong foundation which didn't appear to have crumbled despite not having spoken for years.

'It's so lovely to see you,' said Annabel, taking a seat.

'I can't believe it's been almost five years since we last met. You haven't changed much at all.'

They had a lot to catch up on and their conversation flowed. They talked about old classmates and fond memories from their university days. Becca told Annabel all about the ordeals of her and Adam's marriage and she was excited to talk about her new fiancé, Lucas, who she'd met at a work event. Becca had been writing for a London magazine for a number of years and about eighteen months ago she was promoted to be their culture editor.

'Enough about me. How's life at Herold & Hains?' she asked.

'Great,' said Annabel automatically. That was always her default response when anyone asked her about work. She didn't want to complain, but more importantly she needed to reassure herself that everything was going well. 'Actually, "great" is probably a bit of an overstatement. It's okay.' She went on to tell Becca about Sandra and Annabel's latest disappointment at missing out on the editor's role.

'That sucks.'

'It does, to be honest. But you know me. I'll bounce back. I'm sure there'll be other opportunities soon and it'll be my time. It's just a bit frustrating. All the hard work and not much to show for it.'

'Totally get you. You've always been way more patient than I am. I know I'd be looking elsewhere by now if that was me.'

The skin on the back of Annabel's neck prickled. Becca's words had been echoed by many over the last few weeks and she was finding it harder and harder to push the thoughts to the back of her mind.

'Speaking of which, a friend of mine works at Molière Publishing. I heard they were looking for an editor at the moment. It might be worth a look if you're interested,' said Becca.

'I'm not looking,' said Annabel automatically, before realising she might have sounded a bit defensive. 'But thanks for the tip.' Seeing the expression on Becca's face she added. 'It wouldn't hurt to have a look, I suppose.'

'Exactly. I'll send her details through, and I'll find the link for the job posting. You can see if it's something you'd be interested in. If you are, let me know and I can put in a good word for you. Actually, I might have one of Iona's cards in my purse.'

After some searching, Becca slid a grey and white business card across the table to Annabel. 'She's the recruiting manager. She's really nice.'

'Thanks, I'll have a think about it,' said Annabel, slipping the card into her pocket.

Just as she was leaving the restaurant a text came through from Abi:

I got Wednesday off. I'll see you at the shop at 11. It's on Fulham High Street. Mum said she's coming too x

The text was followed by a link to the shop's website and Annabel typed out a quick reply:

Great! I'll see you both there x

When she got home, Annabel was in high spirits. The evening had gone well, and it was nice to have her friend back in her life. She took off her coat and emptied her pockets, laying the contents on the table including the card Becca gave her earlier and an envelope she forgot was there.

Eagerly she picked the envelope up and opened it, pulling out the small card. *The Christmas wish card.* With everything going on, she had forgotten to go back to the square to hang it on the tree. She was just about to put it in the bin when a thought occurred to her. *St. N.* Remembering the signature on the letter she had received alongside the Advent calendar she thought, *no, that can't be*. 'I hadn't even hung it on the tree,' she said talking to Marley. 'And even if I did, that's not what I'd asked for. These things never come true anyway,' she said discarding the paper.

Her thoughts returning to the business card Becca gave her earlier, she picked it up off the table. She wasn't sure whether she'd apply for the position, but she thought having a look couldn't hurt. After reading through the job posting a couple of times, she had to admit that it did sound like the role she was after; but even the thought of approaching a competitor made her feel disloyal. *Why do I find this so difficult even to consider?* She thought of James's advice. *Maybe he's right. Maybe I should go for it.* Despite feeling the pull to something new, her doubts still had a strong hold on her. *But if I wasn't good enough to get the role at Herold & Hains, why would they pick me somewhere else*? she thought, before shutting down her computer.

The next morning as Annabel sat down at her dining table, her eyes stopped on the business card again. *No.* She was happy at Herold & Hains.

She flicked through Shaw's manuscript, and a feeling crept into her heart: her big break was just around the corner, she was sure of it. Yet despite her optimism, she felt a sense of guilt for squandering an opportunity and felt she was letting James down somehow. But why did she care so much about what James thought? They were just friends, and in the end, she was sure his advice was only that: a friend trying to help another. So, she pushed the card aside and pulled the Advent calendar closer to open the window behind number thirteen.

Accept an invitation or invite someone out

She had no plans to go anywhere so she wasn't sure where she could invite someone out to, but she was excited about the prospect of getting invited somewhere. *I must keep an open mind*, she thought. As she got ready for work, she remembered that it was the day of the book club. She'd enjoyed herself last time; she looked forward to the discussion later and hoped she'd see Alex there again. She grabbed the book off her bedside table and placed it in her bag before leaving the flat.

The train ride into the city was ideal reading time to finish the last few pages. Closing *Before the Coffee Gets Cold*, she looked out the carriage window as it approached its final stop. She remembered Alex's cryptic words at the last event as he had talked about the book: 'It reminded me of the questions I wanted to ask someone if I had the chance to meet them for one last time.' *What did he want to ask and of who?* she wondered. Maybe it wasn't her business to know, but she hoped to find out.

Annabel could hear the burble of excited chat as she approached a group of her colleagues in the office when she arrived.

'That looks gorgeous, Eloise' gushed Sandra, her eyes quickly flicking to the next woman in the circle.

'What are you wearing, Liv?' she asked, probably more keen to tell everyone about her own outfit for the Christmas party.

'Not sure. I think I'll wear the same dress as last year. Haven't had a chance to look for anything else and I only wore that dress once,' replied Liv.

'What about you, Annabel?' asked Sandra as Annabel joined the group.

'I got a new dress the other day, actually. I think I'll wear that,' replied Annabel.

'Can we see it?' asked Sandra.

'I don't have a photo of it, sorry.'

'I've got a picture of mine,' said Sandra eagerly, her cheeks flushing with pleasure at the opportunity to talk about herself. 'Do you want to see it?'

Everyone gathered around Sandra's screen as she pulled up a rather revealing red dress with a low-cut back. Sandra was clearly loving all the attention and was seemingly in a great mood, so Annabel decided it could be a good time to approach her with the proposal about the manuscript.

'Do you have a minute?' she asked Sandra when the others had returned to their desks.

'What's up?'

'I was wondering if you had time to look at my proposal about the manuscript. I've worked out what categories we can slot the book into and how we can use the marketing to make it commercially viable,' said Annabel.

'Oh. Well, I need to get off in a minute, but I'll take a look at it later if that's okay. Just email me what you've got,' said Sandra.

'Sure,' said Annabel, a little disappointed. 'Just let me know what you think.'

Annabel had been running around all day from meeting to meeting. It was nearly five o'clock when she typed out an email to Sandra and attached the proposal clicking send before she shut her laptop down.

She stepped out onto the pavement to see a long queue that snaked around at the bus stop. She knew that getting on at this time might be an impossible mission. She didn't want to miss the start of discussion at the book club so, she decided to walk instead; quickly texting Lucy that she was running late. A couple of streets away she checked the time again: only two minutes to spare. She picked up the pace and jogged the last stretch, just making it there as they were about to start the discussion.

The dialogue was great and everybody enjoyed the book, but Helen was disappointed that there were no second chances, that changing the past didn't change the characters' present.

'It seemed to defeat the purpose,' she said.

'Maybe the purpose wasn't to change the present, but rather to right your reaction. Or maybe to say the things that you wanted to but couldn't or were too afraid to at the time. I suppose it's a way of being able to let go and move on,' said Annabel.

'Perhaps,' said Helen. 'But I still think it would have made the story more interesting if they didn't have that rule.'

Before they ended the conversation Julie asked everyone what book they wanted to read for next month. Since Helen wasn't keen on this month's choice, they were happy to go with her suggestion of *The Night Tiger*.

As Annabel was about to close her book, she pulled on the piece of paper sticking out at the top: the Advent calendar note. She still had unfinished business. She placed the note back in the book and closed it, taking a deep breath as she walked to the other side of the room.

'This was a great suggestion. I really enjoyed it,' she said as she walked up to Alex.

'I'm glad you liked it. It's Annabel, isn't it?'

'I'm sure I could think of a few times when I would have loved the chance to go back and ask someone a question I didn't at the time or say something even if that didn't change a thing,' said Annabel.

'I think we all have these moments of regret.'

'Yes, I remember you saying it last time.'

'I was thinking about my grandmother. I'd have liked to ask her a few questions if I had the chance to speak to her once more,' he said.

She wasn't sure what she was expecting. Maybe an ex-partner or an old friend, but his answer had taken her by surprise, in a good way.

'Were you close?'

'You could say that. I spent quite a bit of time with her when I was younger.'

Annabel was still clutching the book and the piece of paper in her hand. The thought of what she was about to do made her palms sweat and her stomach churn.

'Listen,' she said with a slight tremble in her voice. 'I was wondering if you wanted to go out for some food sometime?' she said quickly. 'It'd be nice to carry on the conversation.'

He smiled, which settled Annabel's nerves a bit.

'Sure. When were you thinking?'

Annabel hadn't thought that far ahead. She was just pleased he didn't say no.

'Erm, I'm free this Saturday evening if that works for you?'

'Let me check my schedule, but Saturday could work,' he replied.

They swapped numbers and agreed to work out the details later.

'What was all that about?' asked Lucy when Annabel returned to pick up her coat.

'Just completed today's task,' said Annabel, smiling as she passed the note to her friend.

***

24 Windows

Annabel sipped her morning coffee with mixed feelings about her day ahead. She'd managed to finish most of her projects, so her workday wasn't promising to be too hectic. Jonathan had given her the afternoon off to get ready for the party later.

The Advent calendar stood proudly on the dining table, and she wondered what little adventure might lie behind the window of number fourteen. Two weeks in, she was almost blasé about each little scroll, in contrast with the internal panic she had at first when she was challenged by a task. She didn't like to admit it, but she was actually looking forward to her morning ritual of unveiling the task behind each window. With an air of confidence, she opened the hatch and read the note.

Do something nice for yourself

She felt almost disappointed reading the message. It didn't sound like much of a challenge. As she got dressed for work, she began to wonder what she could do. *People like to treat themselves to massages and spa days*. She'd never quite had the courage to admit that she hated the thought of lying naked on a table at the mercy of someone else's hands. It seemed more like punishment than a treat for her. *Maybe a manicure*, she thought, looking at her nails. But that didn't feel significant enough to count as a challenge.

After finishing work early, she set off to go home but decided to take a detour. As she walked past a hair salon, she looked at her reflection in the shop window. Suddenly, the perfect opportunity stared back at her. Her curls didn't often see the hands of professionals. Probably partly due to the number of comments she received through the years about her hair being 'far too difficult to style'. *Salons weren't supposed to be a place where you come out feeling worse than when you went in. Especially not when you're paying for the privilege*, she thought. She never felt the need to look like she just stepped off the cover of a magazine or to be made to look like every other woman in London. Besides, she liked the way her hair looked naturally; or at least that's what she told herself.

Scrutinising her reflection, she felt a sudden wave of courage. A spark of confidence that maybe this time she could take control of the situation and get a haircut she actually liked. Without much hesitation, she decided to go in and treat herself to something nice.

'Have you got an appointment?' asked the woman standing behind a computer screen. Annabel couldn't help but notice her rainbow-coloured hair brushed to one side and held in a perfect windswept position by at least half a can of hair spray.

She certainly doesn't try to look like everybody else out there, Annabel thought, blinking quickly before the woman could wonder if she was staring at her.

'I don't, but I was hoping you might have a free slot available.'

'Is it for a cut and dry? If you want colouring as well that won't be possible today, I'm afraid.'

'No colouring. Just a cut and blowdry.'

'We're quite busy, but let me have a look,' she said, before turning back to her screen.

'We might just have a slot. Mia, do you have time before your next one at four?' she asked, turning to one of the other women, who was busy rearranging rows of hair conditioners on the shelves.

'Sure, if it's only a cut and blowdry,' she said as she approached them.

She led Annabel to one of the empty seats and threw a black cape around her.

'I really love your colour. It's not often I see someone with natural colour like yours,' she said to Annabel.

'Thanks,' said Annabel, wondering if the compliment was just part of her service. But regardless, she started to feel at ease.

'How much are we taking off, then?' she asked.

'Not much. About an inch or two from the ends, I think.'

'And how would you like it styling?'

'Not sure really. I'm not keen on having it completely straight, but it'd be nice to have something a bit different. Nothing too extreme, though,' she added quickly.

'Leave it with me. Lou will take you to get your hair washed.'

Hair washing felt like a chore to Annabel on most days, but here she was in for a different experience. Her feet propped up and her scalp massaged, she almost felt she could drift off.

'We're almost done,' said Lou 'I'll just brush through your hair.'

Here we go, thought Annabel bracing herself for the painful tugs of the comb, but before she could wince, she felt the brush effortlessly glide through her hair. She wasn't sure if it was the products they used or the brush itself, but she couldn't remember the last time she didn't want to cry out in pain during a hairdressers' appointment.

Mia worked quickly and although Annabel was slightly nervous as she watched her locks fall to the ground, she somehow trusted that it would look fine in the end. With every snip and comb Mia sculpted her creation and it wasn't long before it was time for the blowdry. The round brush picked up large chunks of Annabel's hair and twirled them into gentle waves which rested on her shoulders. It was a relief when the engine-like sound of the hairdryer stopped buzzing in Annabel's ears, and she could finally see the end result.

'What do you think?' asked Mia, holding a mirror so Annabel could see the back.

She was almost speechless.

'Wow, it looks amazing.'

'I think it really suits you,' she smiled as she unwrapped the cape and led Annabel to the front of the shop.

Walking past a row of shops, Annabel couldn't help but look at her reflection. For once she was pleased with the result. Her flowing amber waves seemed less unruly, and as a bonus, she'd completed the day's task as well.

It was nearly six in the evening when she got home, so she didn't have much time left to get ready. She took the dress out of the wardrobe still in its protective cover and laid it on the bed before jumping in the shower.

Standing in her underwear, drying off the last few drops of water, she stood in front of her bed. As she unzipped the bag the dress was unveiled. She hadn't seen it since she brought it home a week ago, but it was just as she remembered it to be. She carefully pulled the dress over her head and after adjusting the sleeves she attempted to pull the zip up at the back. After struggling for a few seconds, she remembered that she had asked her mother for help when she first tried it on at the shop. But she didn't have anyone around to help today so she had to find another way.

Suddenly she remembered an old trick her Nana Margaret taught her once. She headed to the kitchen and rummaged through the drawers. When she found what she was looking for, she took the dress off and pulled a long piece of thread through the top of the zip.

Putting the dress back on, she held onto the string with one hand and attempted to pull on it. There was a slight movement before the zip stopped midway up her back. *How could Nana make it look so easy?* She tried to pull it up and then down again, but it wouldn't budge. The opening was now too small so she couldn't get out of the dress.

I can't believe this! What am I going to do now? After a couple of further attempts at dislodging the stuck zip she decided it was pointless to keep at it. *I've just got to leave it and ask Liv to help when I get there.*

She tied the belt around her waist and turned to face the mirror. The green chiffon flowed effortlessly, contouring her figure; the skirt stopped just below her knees. The colour almost matched her cat-like eyes, complementing her fair skin that was left uncovered by the short sleeves. Maybe it was the dress or her new hair style, but she felt radiant.

She slipped on a pair of dark emerald-green heels to complete the look. Annabel had been lucky as her skin never required a lot of attention and she preferred to keep makeup to a minimum, only wearing it on special occasions. To her, wearing too much of it was hiding behind a mask, pretending to be someone else. She'd have gone without it on most days, but today felt different. As a finishing touch, she applied a light cover of bronze eye shadow and added a matte auburn lipstick on before she was ready to go. Just as she was about to put her coat on there was a knock on the door.

Who on earth is that?

She opened the door, surprised to find James standing there.

'Wow, you look so different. I mean in a good way, of course. Sorry,' said James, his eyes still firmly fixed on Annabel. 'Is this a bad time?'

His comments took her by surprise. It wasn't so much the words, but the way he said them. She swore she could sense a break in his voice, a slight but noticeable contrast to his usual laid-back demeanour.

'Thanks,' said Annabel with a smile, not entirely sure how else to respond to the compliment. 'I'm heading out to the office Christmas party. My taxi should be here in ten minutes,' she said, checking her phone.

'I just wanted to give this back to you. I've set a few things up on it,' he said, handing her back the watch.

'That's great. Thanks. I almost forgot about it.' Before she could think too much about it, she said, 'Actually, would you mind giving me a hand with the zip on my dress? I think I got it stuck.'

'Sure,' said James stepping inside the flat.

Annabel turned around and lifted her hair as James tried to dislodge the stuck garment. Her heart started to pound faster as she grew more and more conscious of their closeness. She was grateful he couldn't see her face when she felt his fingers brush against her back. Her skin prickled and soon all she could her was her heart thumping loud in her ear.

'There,' said James finally, clearing his throat.

'Thanks,' said Annabel, turning around and hoping her makeup would hide the heat she could feel radiating off her cheeks. Her phone buzzed as the taxi arrived outside.

'That's my cab. I'd better get going,' she said, trying not to look straight at him.

'Yeah. Have a good time,' said James as he left her apartment.

Annabel was pleasantly surprised that the dinner had gone well, and she had been enjoying herself. It was ten o'clock already and people seemed to be having a great time. Decorations hung aloft, compensating for the high ceilings of the room. The band was fantastic, and she had a chance to chat to some people she didn't normally talk to. Her preference for keeping her outside-of-work and professional lives separate meant that she didn't often have personal conversations with her colleagues beyond the courteous, *how was your weekend*?

Liv and Ben were having a great time on the dance floor. Sandra was busy selling raffle tickets across the room, and Annabel found herself warming to her even more. She had a certain charm and Annabel had to admit that her initial reservations about her might have been unfounded. The raffle money was for charity and people found it hard to say no to her. Thomas had been exceptionally generous. The money was for a good cause and there were some great prizes to be won, so she had bought a couple of tickets herself.

Although she was having a great time, Annabel made plans to leave shortly after the tickets were drawn. The office Christmas party's raffle prizes were talked about every year at Herold & Hains.

Even though there was some disappointment, everybody applauded when Liz from accounts won the spa vouchers. Annabel didn't end up empty handed either: her lucky number nineteen was drawn, and she was pleased with her Selfridges gift vouchers. She was sure she'd find a few things there to treat herself.

Soon it was time to draw the final prize. The eagerly anticipated all-expenses-paid weekend away to Rome. It was probably the most extravagant prize they'd ever given away in any year. The number was drawn, but after calling it a few times no one raised their hands. Everybody was frantically looking and hoping it was theirs, but no one claimed it. It was only when Nadia started looking through Sandra's tickets, she realised she'd found the winning one.

'It's here,' she shouted, waving the ticket in her hand. 'It's one of yours, Sandra.'

Even though Sandra's reactions were often over the top, her surprise seemed exaggerated, even more so than usual. It almost felt like it was a well-rehearsed performance, almost Oscar worthy.

'Congratulations,' said Annabel as Sandra returned to the table. 'I wish I was that lucky.'

'It's the Midas touch,' laughed Sandra.

The party was a huge success and Sandra seemed to be in a great mood, especially after her win, so Annabel felt maybe it would a good time to ask if she had a chance to read her proposal yet.

'I did, but I don't think it'll work,' said Sandra. 'There're just too many unknowns and we can't take that risk.'

'But…'

'We should just enjoy ourselves tonight and stop talking about work. We can discuss it next week,' said Sandra, putting an end to their conversation.

After all the prizes were handed out, the band resumed playing and people returned to the dance floor.

'Come on Annabel, just come and dance with me and Ben.'

'Don't feel like it, Liv.'

'Just forget about Sandra and that manuscript for a few hours, will you? Come on and dance with us,' insisted Liv.

'I'd just make a fool of myself up there, but you go and enjoy yourselves.'

'Come on, the music is great and who cares what others might think. You can't do worse than Ronnie's robot routine.

No one pays attention and most of them are drunk already anyway.'

Annabel thought that Liv was probably right and if she'd learnt anything over the last couple of weeks it was that living her life fearing what other people thought of her wasn't much fun. 'All right, I'll come,' she said finally. 'But just because I know you won't stop hassling me until I do.'

Annabel danced around with Liv and Ben and a group of people from Marketing. Liv was right: the music was great. She hated to admit it, but she really enjoyed herself.

As well as the evening had gone, she decided it was time to call it a night when the band took a break.

'I'd better get going, Liv,' said Annabel.

'Already? We were just thinking about heading to a club once they close up here.'

'No clubbing for me. I'm shattered and I've got something on tomorrow. I don't want to get home too late.'

'All right. I hope you had a good night though?'

'I did. It was good fun. You have a good time and I'll see you on Monday,' she said, before heading to the cloak room to collect her coat. As she approached, she heard muffled noises coming from the back of the room but couldn't see anyone at the front. When she stepped closer, she only just caught the back of a conversation.

'Oh, you naughty boy.'

She wasn't sure what was going on, but she instinctively stopped in her tracks and stayed still. She wanted to get her coat but had the feeling she had just walked in on someone.

She was thankful she didn't see anything other than a pair of shiny shoes poking out from under the rows of coats. Keen to avoid any embarrassing encounters, she contemplated turning around and heading back to the room. But she wanted to get going and thought they might have heard her anyway.

She cleared her throat and coughed. She couldn't hear any movement for a second, so she called out: 'Hello, is anybody there?'

Annabel tried hard to hide her emotions when Sandra stepped out from behind a row of coats. She didn't look her usual polished self. Her hair was messy, and a smudge of lipstick sat at the edge of her otherwise perfectly contoured lips.

'Oh, Annabel. Have you been here for long?'

'No, just came to collect my coat. I think I'm done for the night. I'd better get going.'

'So soon. I hope it's not because of what I've said earlier.'

'No, I'm just tired,' replied Annabel. 'Are you okay? You look a bit … flustered.'

'I'm fine. I was just looking for something at the back,' she said, trying to smooth her hair down. 'I think I had a bit too much wine.' Sandra let out a nervous laugh.

'The party was great. Thanks for persisting that I came along.'

'I'm so glad you had a good time.'

Clearly not as good as you.

Well, that was awkward, she thought as she got into the taxi. Annabel despised office gossip and she sure wasn't going to start spreading it, but she found it hard to get rid of the thoughts pushing into her head. She knew it wasn't her business to know but she couldn't help but wonder who the man was behind the curtain.

I'm sure I'll hear about it soon enough.

Just as she managed to shift her attention away from Sandra and the man behind the curtain, her thoughts turned to her encounter with James earlier. As much as it probably didn't mean anything she recounted their short exchange. Did they have a moment or was she imagining things? *It was probably nothing*, she thought as the car passed through the dark streets.

Chapter 7

Annabel didn't get a good night's sleep, tossing and turning for a few hours. Her overactive mind kept her awake and when she finally drifted off, a distorted recollection of memories streamed through.

It was probably the wine, she thought as she woke, not wanting to see too much into the strange dreams.

Keen to keep her drifting mind away from last night's events, she went straight to open a new window on the calendar. She was puzzled as she revealed the day's task. She turned to look out the window and then back to the message. *But it isn't snowing*. After another look at the piece of paper still in her hand there was no mistaking it.

Have a snowball fight

'Well, that's just not possible. How on earth should I make that one happen?'

The weather app on her phone brought a slight glimmer of hope. It did forecast snow, but not until later in the evening.

'There's nothing I can do about this,' she said, leaving the note on the table.

Her date with Alex wasn't until seven in the evening, but she still had to figure out what to wear. It wasn't easy, and she tried not to think of the fact that her dating skills were a bit rusty. She was with David for eight months and they met through a mutual friend. It wasn't like she was actively dating even then. But she had been single for a few years before they met. It was terrifying and embarrassing all at the same time. A bit like that recurring dream she had when she was thirteen; standing at the front of the class trying to recite poetry wearing nothing but her underwear. She needed confidence and something to steady her nerves.

Planning and preparation always eased her anxiety, so she methodically worked through her wardrobe looking for a suitable outfit. She wanted something that said, 'I'm interested but not desperate'. Most of what she found said more like, 'I'm ready to pitch you my brightest idea'.

She pulled out a red lace bodycon dress. *That's a bit much for a first date*, she thought.

After a few more unsuitable outfits, she came across a moss-green A-line knitted dress with a black belt around its waist.

'Perfect. Classy without being too revealing. Just what I was looking for.'

With the dress selected, she decided to go for a walk. The high street was busy with shoppers rushing around. Festive displays drew her eyes from one shop window to the next.

She suddenly stopped in front of one of them. The display gave her an idea. It might not have been the most conventional one, but who said she couldn't get creative?

Scouring the shelves, she grabbed a couple of large boxes and headed to the station. And it wasn't long before she was standing in the front garden of a large semi-detached Edwardian house in Ealing. Peering through the bay window, she spotted Nelly and Ivy playing in the front room. Stepping back a little, she hurled a couple of soft white balls at the glass. The girls ran straight to the window, giggling loudly.

'Girls. What are you up to in there?' came Lucy's voice as she stepped into the room.

'It's not us,' they shouted in chorus. 'It's Aunty Annabel throwing snowballs at the window.'

'Snowballs?' she asked in disbelief as she looked out. 'But it's not snowing?'

'What's going on?' she asked Annabel opening, the window.

Annabel smiled, holding up a full bucket of white plush balls.

'Oh, it must be the calendar,' said Lucy. She wrapped up the children and threw a coat on herself before heading to the back garden where Annabel was waiting for them. They split into teams and built barricades behind a hedge and the playhouse. A continuous shower of white pellets emerged from behind the fortress, ricocheting off the top of the playhouse and falling onto the privet hedge. The girls gave commands amongst a stream of constant laughter.

Annabel thoroughly enjoyed herself and watching Nelly and Ivy reminded her of Abi and her playing in the snow as children. The carefree times when nothing mattered, and they could play from dawn till dusk.

The snowball fight went on for a while before Annabel and Lucy had to declare ceasefire. 'We surrender,' shouted Annabel from behind the barricades, waving a white tissue.

The girls marched back into the house, clearly high on their victory over the adults and went straight to the kitchen for a refuel of biscuits before plotting their next siege.

'That was so much fun,' said Annabel out of breath.

'It was,' said Lucy, putting the kettle on.

It wasn't long before the girls brought the snowballs into the house and carried on their siege one against another in the living room. A look of horror crossed Lucy's face when she heard thuds coming from the room next door.

'Oh my God. I better move my mother's porcelains from the mantelpiece before they end up in bits,' said Lucy, rushing to the next room for a moment.

Lucy and Annabel were soon deep in conversation, but with December in full swing, the days were short, and the dark winter evening was closing in quickly.

'I'd better get going,' said Annabel as she looked at her watch. 'Have to get ready for my dinner with Alex.'

'Almost forgot. Have you decided what you're wearing?'

'Yes. I just need to get home and get changed.'

'Exciting. Hope you have a great time. You can call me later and tell me all about it.'

Nelly and Ivy were still caught up in the game when Annabel headed home, so she decided to leave the props for them to enjoy. The temperature outside had dropped, and she pulled her mittens on while hurrying along the path. Small specs of snow started to drift through the dark air, glinting in the glow of the streetlights as she made her way to the station.

Annabel arrived at the restaurant five minutes early. The hostess asked if she had a reservation and was looking through her list when Annabel spotted Alex sitting at the one of the tables by the window, attempting to adjust his perfectly styled hair in the reflection before looking up to wave at Annabel.

She pretended not to notice for a few seconds before she waved back as the woman showed her to the table.

Alex was well dressed as usual and as he lent in to give her a kiss on the cheek Annabel could smell his aftershave. It was very distinctive and a bit too musky for her liking. She preferred cleaner scents. *At least it's not Brut.*

Annabel couldn't believe her luck that he'd said yes when she asked him out. He had so many faces. An actor, a poet, and he was clearly into fitness as well. He knew what he wanted in life and had the determination to go after it. She'd let him pick the restaurant and she didn't mind his choice even if it was a bit pretentious for her liking.

'This place is great,' said Alex. 'They have a great selection of European wines.'

Annabel had very little knowledge about wine from any country, let alone European ones but she listened with great appreciation as Alex got more into it.

'This would go well with the fish or chicken.' He pointed at an unpronounceable Portuguese wine. 'That reminds me of a time I was travelling around the south of Europe. The food there was amazing.'

Annabel listened intently and asked questions at first, but that just sent Alex down another rabbit hole of tales. After browsing the menu for some time, Annabel still couldn't decide what to have. As discretely as she could, she looked around at other people's plates for inspiration. Most of the dishes seemed to come in tiny portions that reminded her of a dinner with the Borrowers. She chuckled to herself as she imagined Alex shrinking to the size of the saltshaker on the table. He recommended a couple of dishes she wasn't sure about. She preferred no-nonsense restaurants serving authentic food, so she chose a dish that sounded the least pretentious.

The food was delicious, but Annabel was glad she ordered a starter once she saw her next course arrive.

Alex was very confident and was certainly not short on things to say, but by the end of the main course Annabel started to feel like an audience to his performance rather than a participant in a two-way conversation. When she spotted a gap in his monologue, she was keen to change the subject and bring things back onto common ground.

'So, when did you join the book club?' she asked.

'I think it was about four months ago. I used to go to one when I lived in Sydney and I looked for one as soon as I settled in London. I've always loved reading and like to share my experiences with others,' he said.

I bet you do. 'Yes, a story can have so many different layers and it's interesting to hear what others make of something you both read. Like the book you recommended last time.'

'Yes, the story in the café.'

Annabel was still intrigued about what he would have asked his grandmother if he had the chance, but she didn't want to seem nosy. To her luck, Alex was more than happy to share.

'My grandmother always told me stories about wealthy relatives when I was a child. When she passed away I kind of thought she might mention something about an inheritance in her will. I was her only grandchild, you see. But she never did. I was disappointed. If I could speak to her one more time, I'd love to ask her about that.'

She'd expected him to come out with something more sentimental than questions about an inheritance. She sat in silence for a second, pretending to chew her food, trying to work out an appropriate response.

'Maybe she had a diary somewhere. That might have mentioned something about it,' she said finally.

'You could be right. I never thought of that,' he said.

Annabel started to see why Alex might have liked the idea of her asking him out. *It served yet as another proof that no one could resist his charm.*

She remembered Julie trying to tell her something at the end of the book club. *Maybe she tried to warn me about him.* Annabel thought she might have been a bit too ambitious at the start of their date thinking that they'd make it through to dessert.

By the end of the main course, she was regretting not waiting until she'd finished her main. Even chasing the last grain of rice on her plate with her fork felt more interesting than listening to Alex, but he didn't seem to notice. He carried on with his story with Annabel nodding along and occasionally throwing in a 'that's interesting'. All the while, she kept thinking of ways to cut the evening short. But anything that came to her mind seemed rude and quite obvious. So, she braced herself for another thirty minutes of the Chronicles of Alexander the Fascinating before she could extract herself from the situation.

The thought of chocolate raspberry cheesecake was the only thing that kept her going at that stage, along with her mother's strict view on good manners.

As the waiter was about to clear away their dishes, asking if they were ready for dessert, her phone rang.

She scrambled to find it in her purse before the caller could hang up. Just getting to it in the nick of time she answered, sounding slightly exasperated.

'Hello.'

'Hi Annabel, it's James.'

'Oh, hi.'

'Sorry to bother you, but you had a delivery arrive just now and the driver won't leave it outside your door. He said he didn't have authorisation to leave it with a neighbour either, so he was going to take it back to the depot; and he might not be able to deliver it again until later next week. He's here with me now and I was just wondering if you'd be okay with him leaving the package here rather than taking it back.'

'I completely forgot,' exclaimed Annabel, spotting an opportunity to get away before she had to endure another one of Alex's stories. 'That's fine. I'll get there as soon as I can,' she continued.

'You don't have to come straight away. It'll be fine here until tomorrow. Unless you need it tonight, of course.'

'Thanks so much for letting me know. I'll be there in fifteen minutes,' she replied not waiting for James's answer before she ended the call. Trying to mask her relief, she made her excuses, pulled on her coat quickly and headed out of the restaurant.

'Call me,' gestured Alex, looking slightly disappointed as she made her way to the door and into an idling taxi outside. *Probably because he didn't get to finish his monologue.*

Twenty minutes later she stood outside James's door pressing the doorbell. It didn't take long for him to answer.

'That was quick. I was serious when I said you didn't have to come straight away,' he said, looking slightly puzzled. 'Didn't you have somewhere to be? You look like you did.'

'I did, but you couldn't have been better with your timing. Saved me from another thirty minutes of listening to this guy telling me how great he was. And I bet he still can't remember my name. I should have seen the signs really, but it's all water under the bridge now.'

'Sounds like you had a bit of a night. So, you're welcome then, I suppose. Let me get your parcel. Do you need a hand carrying it over to yours? It's quite heavy.'

'Would you mind?'

Annabel went ahead to open the door and James carried the box inside her flat.

'Where do you want me to leave it?'

'Right there's fine.' Annabel gestured at the space next to the coat hooks.

'What's in it, if you don't mind me asking? It's rather heavy.'

'It's twenty kilos of cat litter,' replied Annabel.

James started laughing. 'It must have been bad if you ditched him for cat litter.'

'You won't believe it. I think I just need a break from dating.'

***

On Sunday Annabel planned to finish the remainder of her Christmas shopping and have a relaxing day. She tried to forget about her disaster of a date with Alex, hoping that the day's task would give her the distraction she needed.

Make a gingerbread house

She smiled as she read the note. It had been years since she last made gingerbread biscuits, let alone attempting to construct a house out of confectionery. She quickly found a recipe and checked through the kitchen cupboards to see if she had everything for the bake. She usually had some flour, butter and eggs in, but she wasn't sure about the rest. After rummaging through the shelves and drawers, she found a jar of ground ginger.

'Still need some sugar and golden syrup,' she said, after inspecting all the cupboards. Just as she was contemplating if she should go to the shop to get the missing items, she had an idea. She reached for her phone and dialled. It didn't take more than a couple of rings before Lucy answered.

'How would the girls feel about helping me with some baking this afternoon?' Annabel asked.

'I'm sure they'd love to give you a hand. But they might be more enthusiastic about the eating part rather than the making. What are you baking?'

'A gingerbread house,' said Annabel. 'I'm also missing a couple of the ingredients for the recipe. I've got some flour, butter and eggs, but not much else.'

'I see. Text me what you need, and I'll see what I've got lying around here. I can bring some decorations as well.'

'Perfect. Just come over whenever.'

'Great. We'll be there in an hour, and you can tell me all about your date with Alex.'

The continuous ring of the doorbell an hour or so later signalled to Annabel that her visitors had arrived. The girls sprinted to the front room, chasing after Marley whilst Annabel took the bags from Lucy and hauled them into the kitchen.

'What have you brought?' she asked. 'I only needed a few things.'

'Just a couple of bits. Had a large box full of cake decorations left over from Ivy's party. Got some edible fairy dust too that the girls insisted on bringing to sprinkle over the house,' said Lucy as she placed the items on the table.

'Yummy. Right girls, who wants to help me bake some gingerbread biscuits?' asked Annabel.

'Me, me!' The girls came running.

After some discussion they decided to make double the amount of dough just in case they needed more pieces, and both Nelly and Ivy insisted on having their own bowls to mix. It wasn't easy getting a five-year-old and a three-year-old to concentrate on the task at hand, but somehow they managed to create two balls of dough. Annabel decided to take charge of cutting out the pieces for the house to avoid any wobbly lines and with enough dough left over they agreed that the girls could shape the smaller pieces later.

The first batch had gone into the oven and was ready by the time they finished cutting out the figures. They left the trays to cool on the countertop; the spicy scent of freshly baked biscuits filling the air. Nelly and Ivy found it difficult to resist the bronze Christmas treats, but they were assured that they could try some of the figures later.

'Are you going to tell me about your date with Alex, then? I'm dying to know how it went,' said Lucy as they sat down with a hot drink, the girls playing with Marley.

'It was awful.'

'Awful? Why, what happened?'

Annabel proceeded to tell Lucy all about the ordeals of the evening and how instead of a sentimental guy, Alex had turned out to be a pompous gold digger.

Lucy burst out laughing. 'Sorry, I know it's not funny. I just didn't expect that.'

'Tell me about it. And I bet he still doesn't know my name.'

'I'm sorry you didn't have a good night. I was really hoping it went well.'

'Yeah, me too. James saved me in the end.'

'James? Was he there, too?'

'No. I was losing the will to live when he rang about a parcel I ordered. So, I pretended it was something urgent and I had to get off. He was like a knight in shining armour.'

'Knight in shining armour, ha?' said Lucy with a grin.

'On, stop that Lucy. He's just a friend. Besides, I've had enough of dates for a while,' said Annabel just as the timer sounded, signalling that the second batch of biscuits was ready to come out of the oven.

After a few minutes on the rack, the first batch was cool enough so Nelly and Ivy could finally try them. Pacified by the sugary treats, they were more willing to partake in assembling the house. The walls went up and were left to set before they decorated the trees and the gingerbread men. The roof was left to be added on last.

'What do you think?' asked Annabel, admiring the build as she munched on another biscuit.

'It's not finished yet,' protested the girls.

'I know, but we'll have to wait until tomorrow before I can add more decorations. It needs to set properly first.'

Nelly seemed disappointed that she couldn't cover the house in edible fairy dust. Ivy didn't seem to mind it much; she was more focused on polishing off another Christmas tree.

'We have quite a few biscuits left. Maybe we could take some over to Mr Adler. He lives just down the hall and I'm sure he'd love to try them,' suggested Annabel.

'Sounds like a lovely idea, doesn't it, girls? But we'd better get going after that. It's getting late.'

They packed up a small box of gingerbread to take home and a few pieces in a separate box for Mr Adler before heading out the door.

James's door opened as they walked past.

'Something smells nice,' remarked James, shutting the door behind him.

'We baked some biscuits,' said Ivy proudly.

'Ginger biscuits,' added Nelly.

'I can smell it,' said James.

'This is Lucy,' said Annabel, introducing her friend.

'Hi,' said Lucy.

'I'm Nelly,' Lucy's eldest introduced herself. 'And this is my sister, Ivy.'

'I'm James,' he said smiling.

'Are you Annabel's boyfriend?' Nelly asked James.

'Nelly,' said Lucy.

Annabel's cheeks turned red. Sensing her discomfort, James said quickly, 'We are just friends.'

'But she said you were her knight,' insisted Nelly.

'Did she?' Laughed James, fixing his eyes on Annabel.

'It was just a figure of speech. I told Lucy you saved me last night. Like a knight in shining armour,' Annabel said her cheeks still hot.

'I see.' Smiled James.

'We better get going. We are delivering some of the biscuits to Mr Adler,' said Annabel, keen to extract herself from the situation.

'I better go as well,' said James. 'It was lovely to meet you all.'

'Bye,' said the girls in chorus as they made their way down the corridor.

The biscuits were well received.

'Please do come in,' Mr Adler said to them, insisting on giving the girls a box of chocolates in return.

'We'd love to, but we can't stay, I'm afraid. These two need to be in bed in an hour,' said Lucy.

'I'll come in for a bit,' said Annabel.

Lucy and the girls waved goodbye, and Mr Adler seemed cheerful as Annabel joined him inside his flat. The faint sound of music streamed into the hallway from the living room.

'What are you listening to today?' asked Annabel. 'Sounds kind of jazzy.'

'I was in the mood for something a bit different. It's the great Henry Mancini. He really knew how to write good music. A lot of them did back then. Not like today's mish mash. Handsome chap too, Dotty always said.'

'I recognise this one,' said Annabel as *Moon River* came on.

'Dotty loved Audrey Hepburn signing it. I had a record of it somewhere, but I'm not sure where it went.'

They sat talking for a while and Mr Adler enjoyed a couple of ginger biscuits with his tea. Annabel politely refused. She had started to feel sick after eating too many earlier.

'Your wife must have been a lovely woman,' she said. 'I wish I had met her.'

'I'm sure you'd have got on well with her. She was one of a kind. Could light up any room she walked into.'

Annabel didn't want to pry, but she was intrigued.

'How did you two meet?' she asked.

'At a ballroom dance in central London. At the Lyceum. It's not a dance hall anymore, but the building is still there. I can still remember seeing her when I walked in. I knew right then and there that I had to get a dance with her.'

In the way he talked about his wife, the life they'd lived and the places they visited together, his love for her was still ever-present, even after so many years. He reminded Annabel of the penguins she used to see in the wildlife park. *They weathered the storms together.*

As she listened to his story, she wondered about her own life. Her history of failed relationships and her latest fail with Alex didn't fill her with hope. She wondered if she'd ever feel love like Mr Adler and his wife had or if that feeling was now only reserved for romantic stories.

***

Annabel tried to act normal when she arrived at work on Monday morning. Sandra was already in a meeting, which made it easier to steer clear of awkward conversations, but Annabel knew she couldn't avoid her forever. Liv was keen to tell her how their night unfolded after she'd left the party, but with her mind on other things, Annabel found it hard to concentrate.

'Are you okay?' asked Liv.

'Yes, I'm fine. Just a bit tired, that's all.'

'Tired after the weekend? Didn't you have your date on Saturday? It must have gone well, then,' said Liv with a grin.

'Don't even go there, Liv. It was an utter disaster. I'll tell you about it later, but we'd better go now. They're heading over to room five.'

Sandra kept glancing in Annabel's direction during the Monday morning meeting. At first it was just a bit odd, but after a while it started to unsettle Annabel. *I wish she would stop looking at me.* She tried to slip out of the room when the meeting finished, but Sandra cornered her as the others were leaving.

'I still feel a bit embarrassed about last Friday,' said Sandra.

'What do you mean?' asked Annabel.

'You know, at the cloakroom.'

'Oh, don't mention it. I wouldn't want to stop anyone having a good time.'

Sandra laughed nervously as Thomas walked past them. Annabel's eyes were drawn to his shoes. It was hard not to look. They were so shiny you could almost see your reflection in them. At that moment she was certain who the person was with Sandra that night behind the curtain of coats.

When Annabel looked up, Sandra's face said it all.

'I can explain,' whispered Sandra instinctively.

'You and him?' Annabel tried hard not to sound judgemental, but it was difficult not to. 'He's married, Sandra. And you work together.'

'Keep your voice down, please. I know. We didn't mean for it to happen.'

'How long have you two been…' She trailed off trying to find the right words. 'How long has this been going on for?'

'Erm… only a couple of weeks. We were going to end things, but then one thing led to another at the party. It was a mistake, Annabel. Please don't say anything to anyone.'

I can't believe this. 'I hate keeping secrets. I'm a terrible liar, you know.'

'You don't have to lie, just don't say anything. Please, I'm begging you.'

Annabel stayed quiet for a while as she digested Sandra's revelation and her plea. *I really don't want to deal with this.*

'I'll do anything. Just please don't say anything to anyone about this,' pleaded Sandra.

Anything. The word struck something in Annabel. She didn't want to be part of this whole thing, but this might be her best chance. 'Fine. I won't say anything, but only on two conditions.'

'Anything.'

'You've got to stop this or come clean. If you two are a thing, he'd better tell his wife and you'd have to be open about it in the office too. You know what happens when you try to hide things like this. People start talking.'

'Sure. I promise I'll sort it. And what's the second condition?'

'That you take another look at my proposal,' said Annabel firmly.

'I told you; it won't work.'

'Just take another look at it. I know it would. Please. Another look is all I'm asking.'

'Fine. But I can't promise that we can go with it. I'd need to convince Thomas of that too.'

'Well, I'm sure that wouldn't be a problem,' said Annabel.

Annabel hated secrets and felt that by keeping one she became an accomplice in some way. She didn't want to know any of this but had no choice in the matter. The weight of knowing was thrust upon her. She had questions she couldn't answer, but equally she didn't want to ask, and she couldn't be sure Sandra was being honest with her either. But there was a glimmer of hope that Sandra would come through on her promise and would at least reconsider her proposal too.

'What was all that about?' asked Liv as she returned to her desk.

'What do you mean?'

'You and Sandra. Things looked a bit intense between you two.'

'Oh, it was nothing. She spilled a drink on my dress at the party and she was still feeling bad about it.'

'When? I didn't see that.'

'It was just as I was leaving.'

Annabel felt awful about lying, but she made a promise and she had to trust that Sandra would stay true to her word and sort things out. She tried hard not to ruminate over her revelation, and thankfully work kept her busy during the day, but the thought of having to dodge Sandra and Thomas for the next few days filled her with dread.

With still a few holidays left for the year, Annabel emailed Jonathan to see if she could take the rest of the week off. She still had a couple of personal things to take care of before Christmas and she felt she could use a few days away from the drama.

Snow was forecast in the evening but only a few tiny specs had fallen by the time Annabel arrived back home. She drew the curtains in the living room and threw her post on the dining table. Marley stretched his legs as he got up from his snug and headed to the kitchen, signalling that it was time for his next meal.

With Marley pacified, Annabel's thoughts turned to her own dinner. She wasn't in the mood for cooking. Resigned to the thought of tinned soup and a fish finger sandwich, she opened the fridge door. She took out a plastic container with a sticky note on the lid.

Shepherds' pie, she read the note with delight.

She must have sneaked this in yesterday when I wasn't looking. Lucy always had a way of looking after her friend without making Annabel feel like she needed it.

Glad she didn't have to think about dinner, Annabel took a dish out and turned the oven on. With not much else to do whilst the food warmed up, she pulled out one of the chairs at the dining table and sat down. The Advent calendar stood in front of her as she scanned through the numbers. It was only then she saw the closed window of number seventeen.

How could I forget? she thought, reaching for the scroll.

Take a leap of faith

I suppose I've already taken a leap of faith with Sandra today, trusting that she'll sort things out.

Her attempts to forget about their earlier chat were made easier by having a lot to do during the day, but once she returned home her mind kept wandering.

Sandra said this *thing* between her and Thomas only started a couple of weeks ago, but Annabel remembered seeing them acting strangely before that. She wondered if this had been going on for longer than what she was letting on.

Did Thomas have a hand in Sandra's promotion? Annabel hated even having the thought. *Don't be stupid!* She was sure that Sandra got the job based on her merits and Thomas had nothing to do with any of it, but the what-ifs kept pushing in.

The business card from Becca still lay on the table. A tantalising reminder of an opportunity. She liked her job at Herold & Hains, and it was true she was frustrated with her lack of progression, but she didn't want to throw the towel in. Not now. Not over this. At the same time, she was curious about a new possibility. *Maybe I could send my CV in. There's no harm in that. They probably wouldn't even interview me anyway.*

After some toing and froing, she started to scroll through Molière Publishing's website. Annabel liked their ethos and sustainability pledges and felt this might be a company she could work for. Finally, an employer that wasn't just about profits.

They supported underrepresented writers from less privileged backgrounds and invested a large proportion of their profits into communities by supplying libraries with books and working with educational charities in less developed countries. Supporting literacy in young people and enabling them to enjoy the worlds stories created was something Annabel felt strongly about. Herold & Hains might have their chic central London offices, could boast about publishing the newest books of well-known writers and offer attractive benefit packages to their staff, but it felt like a cold façade in contrast to the worthy cause Molière Publishing stood for.

Eagerly, she looked through the job posting again and an hour later she had updated her CV, written a cover letter and was about to hit 'submit' on her application. She was ready to take a leap of faith.

Here goes nothing, she thought as she clicked 'apply'.

Chapter 8

Annabel was glad to take a few days off work. She was pleased that she could avoid Sandra for a while, and she still hadn't got over her guilt about submitting her CV for the job. After a well-deserved lie in she was ready to start her day.

When she opened the curtains, the room lit up at once with a flood of brilliant white light. She had to squint, giving her eyes time to adjust to the sight. It was as if the world outside had been transformed overnight. It had stopped snowing, but shimmering specks still floated through the cold air like tiny fish scales.

She couldn't remember the last time she had seen snow like that in the city. Pure, heavy and untouched. Not like the slush they had become accustomed to over the years. The monochrome scene continued as far as her eye could see, a stark contrast to the usual colour-filled chaos of life.

She felt a childlike excitement come over her. Having proper snow was one thing but having it just before Christmas made it even more brilliant. She put on her radio in the kitchen while she made coffee and danced along to the festive tunes. As she sat down at her dining table, she eagerly reached to open the next window on her calendar.

Spend some time in nature

Perfect. With no work for the rest of the week, she couldn't have chosen a better day to spend some time outdoors. Although she had a few things planned for the days ahead, for now they could wait. She was determined to enjoy being present.

Soon she was standing in her hall wearing a long winter coat, wrapping a sage-green knitted scarf around her neck. With her snow boots and hat on, her woollen gloves were the last things she pulled on.

'I'm ready.'

Marley glanced at her with disinterest before he made his way back to the comfort of his snug. Something occurred to her as she stood there in the hallway. She headed back to the living room to a cabinet by the window, opening the drawers one by one.

'There they are,' she said as she took out a couple of things. She put them in her bag on her way out and closed the door.

There was a cold but calm atmosphere when she stepped outside. The faint winter sun softened the air and surrounded everything in its pale glow as she walked through the gate.

The snow crunched under her feet. It lay untouched around her. The low-lying fog hung heavy, constricting the ground. Above, dark branches sagged under their icy blanket. She walked around the park, taking in the transformation. It was the depth of winter and life seemed scarce around her. A couple of robins hopped from one holly bush to another. White flakes fell from the dark green leaves. In the distance, deer roamed the grounds, leaving faint imprints in the snow.

The landscape was vast and still so delicate, as if it was painted on a postcard. Scouring the white plains, she spotted a bench by the lake and headed towards it. It was only faintly visible under the thick layer of snow. Brushing it off, she sat down.

She inhaled the cold air looking over the lake. She couldn't see a soul for miles. As the noises around her grew fainter, soon the only thing she could hear was the sound of her own heartbeat. Taking in the sights, her body entered a state of ease. Her muscles softened and her breathing became smooth and slow. Even though she wasn't far from the hustle and bustle, it was as if she was the only living thing around. She gazed at the vast sheet of white around her and reached into her bag, taking out an unlined notepad and a small pack of pastels. She hadn't drawn for a long time. It was one of those things she once loved but gave up in favour of more meaningful pastimes like building a career. For a second she hesitated, but when her first stroke hit the pad, her hand followed a familiar motion deeply engrained in her subconscious, a habit that years of abstinence couldn't erase. It didn't take long before she was completely lost in the flow. She could have sat there for minutes or hours and she wouldn't have known.

'I see you had a similar thought this morning,' a man's voice broke the silence.

Annabel flinched. Absorbed in the act of creation, she hadn't heard the man approach.

'I'm sorry, I didn't mean to startle you.'

'It was so quiet. I wasn't expecting anyone to be around,' replied Annabel.

'I must remember to carry a bell with me next time.' Smiled James. 'That looks great, by the way,' he said gesturing at the drawing in Annabel's hand as he sat down next to her.

'Thanks. I haven't done this in a while, but everything looked so serene this morning and it felt so good getting lost in the flow again.'

'It's nice to rediscover long-lost passions,' said James. 'So how are things with the calendar?' he asked. 'Have you got any closer to finding out who sent it to you?'

'Not really. Mum was adamant that she didn't, and she seemed genuine about it. I thought it might have been David, but after a few tasks it was apparent that he couldn't have done it either. And then at some point I had a crazy thought that a wish I'd made somehow manifested it…' said Annabel, laughing. 'So I'm no closer, but I'm not too fussed about it anymore. I'm just trying to enjoy each day as it comes.'

'That's a good attitude to have in general, I suppose,' replied James. 'And how is the project going at work?'

'Don't even ask,' said Annabel. 'I worked it out how we can make the original concept work, but Sandra didn't seem interested about it.'

'Eto pozor,' said James.

'Pardon?'

'It means 'that's a shame' in Russian.

'I didn't know you spoke Russian,' said Annabel surprised. 'A man of many talents.'

'Ha-ha. That's an exaggeration. So you really liked that original concept.'

'I do. It's different. Anyway, she said she'd take another look. So I'm not giving up just yet.'

They sat on the bench talking for some time.

'So, tell me something… and please don't take this the wrong way,' said James after a while. 'You're smart, attractive, and you don't have a bad sense of humour either. How come someone hasn't snapped you up yet?'

Annabel wasn't sure whether to be flattered or insulted by the remark. *Is he implying there's something wrong with me?* But before her insecurities could get the better of her, she quickly decided to go with being flattered.

'Thank you, I suppose. But to answer your question, I just haven't had much luck lately. First David, now this latest disaster with Alex. I just think I'm better off being on my own for now. Life is just less complicated that way.'

'Seems fair, I suppose. But you might change your mind when you meet the right person,' said James with a smile.

'Doesn't seem likely, based on my track record. At least not for a while.'

Annabel wondered for a moment why he seemed so interested in her love life. Or rather the lack of it. The odd fluttering sensation in her stomach – vaguely familiar from the other day – took her by surprise. She was quick to dismiss the out of place feelings and turned to him.

'What about you? Now that I think of it, I don't think I've seen you with anyone since you moved in.'

'I didn't know you kept tabs on me,' said James.

Annabel felt her cheeks turn warmer. She was just about to apologise when James went on.

'I'm only kidding.' He smiled at her, and slight dimples emerged on his cheeks. 'Traveling a lot for work and serious relationships don't tend to go hand in hand. And I didn't really feel the need to find someone. I was happy on my own.'

'Was?'

'I don't know. Things might be changing. It's early days, but we'll see where things go,' said James, his smile broadening.

Annabel's phone rang, interrupting their chat. 'Sorry,' said Annabel, before answering the call.

'Hi, I'm looking to speak to Miss Annabel Tate,' came the voice on the other end of the phone.

'Speaking.'

'Hi Annabel, it's Iona Lewis from Molière Publishing. I'm calling regarding your application for our editor position.'

'Oh, hello.' Annabel's voice broke slightly as her pulse quickened.

Sensing it was time to move on, James stood up from the bench and whispered, 'I'll leave you to it.'

Annabel watched as he walked away, listening to the voice on the other end of the phone.

'I've reviewed your CV and your submission, and I was wondering if you'd be available to come in for an interview this week?' asked Iona.

'This week?' Annabel hesitated for a moment, trying to work out what she should say. *Why did I even say that?* Before she could overthink things, her response came almost automatically. 'Sure, I should be available on Thursday if that works.'

'That would be great. Could you be here at 9 a.m.?'

'Yes. That should be no problem.'

'Great. I'll send the details over tonight. Look forward to seeing you then.'

When she hung up the phone, Annabel was in a daze, her heart pounding with excitement. *What just happened?* When she applied for the job, the prospect of an interview seemed far-fetched. But not anymore. With dress-fitting plans for the next day, she only had the afternoon to prepare, so she didn't want to waste any time getting back to her flat.

She reviewed her CV and the job description again, trying to come up with answers to all the possible questions she could think of. She studied the publisher's website again and their repertoire of recently published books. She updated her portfolio of projects she had worked on over the years and did her reading on her interviewer.

As she closed her laptop, a nagging thought occurred to her. If any of what had happened between Sandra and Thomas came out, and they found out that she knew about it, her reference might be at jeopardy. Her earlier sense of being in control soon dissipated, leaving an anxious feeling behind.

Annabel had had a restless night, tossing and turning. At six o'clock she finally decided to stop trying to go back to sleep and sat up in bed. She still had plenty of time before meeting Abi and their mother later that morning, but she couldn't stop thinking about her interview the following day.

Sitting in the dark, she wondered if yesterday's events were all a dream. She checked her calendar. The appointment was there. She still couldn't quite believe she'd been called in for an interview at Molière Publishing. Her, Annabel Tate. *If things go well, I could become an editor.* But that was a big 'if' and she didn't feel she could allow herself even the possibility of the thought at this point. Not after what happened with the promotion and not until she heard from Sandra that the affair was over or that they'd come clean. First, she needed to focus on her interview. Her emotions seemed to change from excitement one minute to guilt and trepidation the next. Determined not to let negativity get the better of her, she decided to take things as they came and stop ruminating over them.

She hadn't seen her sister in months, and she couldn't recall the last time they had spoken before last week. A twinge of guilt bit into her at the thought of her lack of help with Abi's wedding preparations. *But I'll be there for her now.* She was quick to drown out the intrusive thoughts before they had chance to take over. Abi's train was due in at eleven and they had arranged to meet at the dress shop in the city. Once they got the dress fitting sorted the plan was to meet their mother for lunch, leaving Annabel plenty of time to prepare for her interview the next day. Almost ready to go, she nearly forgot to open the window on the calendar. She quickly grabbed the scroll and headed for the door as she unrolled it.

Stand up for what you believe in

Annabel always had a strong sense of who she thought she was, and what she felt was right and wrong, but she wasn't the type to join rallies or protest with others. In a debate over dinner with some friends, she wasn't afraid to voice her opinion, but she was certainly no Rosa Parks. Not sure how she was going to complete this task, she hoped an opportunity would present itself during the day. With that thought she headed into the city.

Annabel's train was on time and a text came in from Abi just as she turned the last corner:

I'll be there in 2 mins x

No rush. I just got here, she replied, and it wasn't long before she spotted Abi approaching her.

'Hey! It's so good to see you,' said Abi, hugging her sister. 'Let's go in, it's freezing out here.'

After sorting out the details the shop assistant disappeared into the back and Abi and Annabel took a seat in one of the private rooms. Annabel was keen to find out how the wedding preparations were going, and Abi wanted to know all about her sister's job.

'So how is it going at the publishing house?' asked Abi.

'It's going well. I've started to work on this new project, which is really exciting, but it's early days.'

'That's great. Sorry you didn't get the editor job. Mum told me about it.'

'It's okay. There will be another opportunity soon, I'm sure,' said Annabel. Not wanting to jinx things, she thought it was best not to mention anything about her upcoming interview.

'And I'm sorry about David, too. I should have called, but I didn't want to make things worse,' said Abi.

'It's okay, Abi. It's not like I have been around or called much lately either,' said Annabel, turning to her sister.

'But you're here now and that's all that matters,' said Abi, squeezing her sister's hand.

'Can't believe you're getting married,' said Annabel. 'My little sister.'

'Stop it. I'll get all emotional.' Abi smiled. 'I really hope you're going to like the dress,' said Abi, just as the shop assistant returned with it in her hand. This was the first time Annabel had seen her bridesmaid's dress. Her mother had told her all about it in great detail, but it wasn't how she'd imagined it. Peach wasn't exactly her colour; it accented her fair skin and not in a good way. But this was Abi's big day, and she wasn't going to make a big deal, or in fact, any deal out of it. The shop assistant ushered her into one of the changing rooms, and drew the curtain behind her.

'Let me know if you need a hand,' said Abi.

The satin felt cold against Annabel's skin as she pulled the dress on. Strangely, there was no mirror in the cubicle, so she couldn't really see what the dress looked like on her, but she had a feeling that it wasn't exactly flattering and could feel that it was loose in places.

'Have you got it on?' asked the shop assistant after a few minutes.

'Mostly,' said Annabel. She drew back the curtains and stepped out, holding the skirt up to stop it from sweeping the floor.

'Could you turn around, please?' asked the shop assistant.

'What do you think?' asked Abi. 'I hope you don't hate it.'

'Of course, I don't hate it. It's lovely,' said Annabel.

'We need to take it in at a couple of places, but it won't take long,' the shop assistant reassured them.

'How're the wedding plans?' asked Annabel.

'Everything seems to be on track, but I can't help worrying that something will go wrong in the last minute.'

'Stop fretting. You're one of the most organised people I know. I'm sure everything will be perfect. Just enjoy it.'

'Hunter said the same thing. He's so laid back. I think that's what freaks me out.' Abi laughed. 'I still can't believe you're coming up for Christmas,' said Abi as she sat back into her chair.

'I know. I just hope mum's going to be on her best behaviour.'

'Me and Dad will make sure she is. Don't you worry. I'm just so glad to have you celebrate with us. I've missed you.'

'Me too,' said Annabel smiling. 'You'll never guess who I'd met the other day.'

'Who?'

'Becca Mirren,' said Annabel.

'Oh, how's she doing?' asked Abi.

'Really well. She is a culture editor for this Magazine in London.'

'Sounds glamorous. Is she still with…' started Abi but realising it might have been a difficult topic for her sister she stopped.

'Adam,' Annabel finished her question. 'It's okay. And no, they'd split up a while back.'

'Oh, really?'

'Yeah, apparently he had an affair.'

'Sounds like you've dodged a bullet,' said Abi.

'I know.'

True to her word, the shop assistant quickly pinned up the dress ready for sewing and agreed that Annabel would come back after Christmas to check the final fit. After agreeing a date, they headed to the restaurant to meet Evelyn.

'Your hair looks lovely, Annabel. Have you done something to it?' Evelyn said as she took off her coat.

'I knew there was something different about you,' said Abi.

'Thanks, Mum. Had it done on Friday for the Christmas party.'

'Oh, how was it? Did you wear the dress we picked out? It was such a gorgeous outfit. You should have seen it, Abi.'

Her encounter with Sandra still firmly in her mind, she quickly answered. 'It was good. I didn't stay for long but had a good time.'

'So have you managed to sort the dress out today?'

'Yes. Annabel looks so lovely in it,' said Abi.

'They've got it pinned up and ready to sew. It should be ready for the final fitting after Christmas,' said Annabel.

'You'll never guess who Annabel met that other day, Mum,' said Abi.

'Who?'

'Becca Mirren.' said Annabel.

'Oh, she got married to Adam, didn't she?' asked Evelyn.

'Yes. But they'd split up a while back,' said Annabel.

'Oh, that's such a shame. He was a nice young man.'

'Mum!' said Abi firmly, shooting their mother an unimpressed look.

'Sorry. I didn't mean it like that,' said Evelyn.

A memory flashed through Annabel's mind. When her and Adam broke up all those years ago and she told her mother about it, her mother's first response was that Adam wasn't unreasonable for wanting Annabel to move back up north with him. Annabel felt she put the blame on her for the breakup. She didn't say it directly, but Annabel could sense the less-than-subtle hint. Annabel could feel herself getting swept up in the emotion she felt back then. Her heart broken and her mother implying it was her fault, but she didn't want to go down that spiral again, so she took a deep breath before she spoke again.

'It's okay,' said Annabel calmly. 'People are not always as they seem to be, Mum. He went off with another woman.'

'Really? That's awful,' said Evelyn.

'Annabel dodged a bullet there, Mum,' said Abi, sensing her sister's unease.

'Sounds like it. But that's all in the past,' said Annabel, managing a smile.

Although it still hurt to think about what happened back then, Annabel knew there was no point in dragging up the past. But going forward she had to be clearer with her boundaries when it came to her mother, and she had to be firm with her if she ever overstepped.

Annabel asked about the plans for the holidays and Evelyn said her dad, George would pick her up from the station in Northallerton to save her the taxi journey on Christmas Eve. She checked her phone as an email flashed up.

Can we talk?

Annabel thought it was best to do this face-to-face and after checking her watch she thought she still had plenty of time to get to the office and back and get an early night before the interview the next day. She typed out a quick reply.

Abi's and Evelyn's train was leaving soon, so after finishing their meal they said their goodbyes and Annabel headed to Herold & Hains.

By the time Annabel got the office, most of the people had left. Liv was just packing up her bag as she spotted her.

'What are you doing here?' she asked. 'Aren't you supposed to be on holiday?'

'Just came to pick something up,' said Annabel. 'Is Sandra still about?'

'She was here a minute ago. Probably gone to another meeting with Thomas. It's like that's all they ever do. Anyway, I've got to go.'

Annabel waited around a couple of minutes, but Sandra was nowhere to be seen. Her computer screen was unlocked, and Annabel rolled over on her chair to check Sandra's calendar to find out where she'd gone. She felt a sense of unease as she opened the calendar on Sandra's email client. No appointment was scheduled as far as Annabel could see, so she flicked the screen back to the inbox as she'd found it.

She was about roll away when she spotted an email folder that caught her eye. *D. Henderson.* Taking a quick look around to see if anybody was around, she opened the folder. The emails were dated from when Sandra started at Herold & Hains. Her eyes darted from line to line as she read the contents.

'I don't believe this,' she said, her heart pounding faster and faster.

She pressed print on a couple of the emails before rushing to the printer to retrieve them. She re-read the lines again and again.

'This is insane.'

Sandra was still nowhere to be seen, so Annabel sat back down at Sandra's desk and scrolled through some more recent emails in her inbox. It wasn't long before her eyes stopped on one of them. Opening the email, she read the lines again and again. She could feel her skin prickle and anger rising from the pit of her stomach.

Her hand was shaking as she pressed print on the email. She stood to get the printout and she froze as she saw Jonathan standing at the printer, lifting off the piece of paper. An ice-cold sensation spread through her core.

His facial expression changed as his eyes scrolled over the lines on the paper. 'What is this?' he mumbled, not realising that Annabel approached. 'Oh, Annabel,' he said, startled. 'I didn't know you were in today.'

'I wasn't, just came to pick something up.'

'Have you seen Sandra anywhere?' he asked.

'No. Is there something wrong?'

'You could say that,' said Jonathan gripping the piece of paper before setting off in the direction of Thomas's office.

Annabel followed behind.

He raised his hand just about to knock when he heard voices from inside. 'Oh, what the hell,' he said, swinging the door open. 'What is going on?' he exclaimed.

Thomas and Sandra froze like rabbits caught in headlights, scrambling to pull their clothes on.

'We need to talk,' Jonathan said firmly. 'Gather yourselves and I want to see both of you in my office now.'

'You devious little…' snarled Sandra, walking towards Annabel.

'Sandra,' growled Jonathan. 'Annabel had nothing to do with this. You only have yourself to thank for what's to come.'

'Annabel, you go home,' said Jonathan calmly, turning to her.

The blood had drained out of Annabel's face as she stood there. Her feet were rooted to the ground, and she could feel a huge lump in her throat as she opened her mouth to speak.

'I just need to ask Sandra something if I may,' she said quietly.

Jonathan gestured for her to go ahead.

'How do you know David?'

Sandra's face changed, her eyes narrowing. 'That's none of your bloody business,' she retorted.

'Watch your language,' interjected Jonathan.

'You took him away from me,' screamed Sandra as she looked Annabel up and down.

Annabel felt a jolt in her chest followed by waves of anger rising from her core. 'So that's why you applied for the job here? To get to me?'

'Ha, you think so much of yourself, don't you? Little Miss Perfect. It was too good an opportunity to miss. It was just a bonus that I could keep an eye on you as well.'

'I don't believe a word you say, Sandra,' retorted Annabel. 'And what was your plan? To undermine me and somehow weasel your way back into David's life?'

'Weasel? He loved me. I just needed him to see it. He deserves so much better than you,' hissed Sandra, her eyes ablaze with rage. 'I knew it was only a matter of time before you messed it all up. Like all other relationships, this would become another victim of your career obsessed life. I just had to wait.'

Annabel's skin fizzed, she could feel her body tremble. A month ago, she would have been instantly swallowed up by self-doubt at the sound of such accusations, but today she had some perspective. Though Sandra's words cut deep, she knew she had the power to change the narrative. She was capable and strong and needed no one but herself to see that. She took a deep breath before she spoke again. 'How did you even get a job here? You never worked in book publishing. You said it yourself,' said Annabel calmly.

'Thomas,' mumbled Jonathan in a daze. 'I told you I wasn't sure about her, but you pushed for Sandra to be hired,' he said turning to Thomas. 'Why? Were you in on this whole thing?'

'It was just a favour for a friend. We needed another editorial assistant in the team anyway and Sandra seemed capable enough,' replied Thomas, the extent of Sandra's deceit dawning on him.

Annabel stood there for a moment, not sure how to feel. Thoughts swirled in her head. 'That's why you told me that my idea was too risky when I applied for the editor role. You stole my pitch and used it to sabotage my career,' she said finally, waiving a printout of an email. 'But how did you know it would work?'

'It was easy. Thomas told me what the panel was looking for and your pitch was practically perfect,' said Sandra.

Jonathan's eyes turned to Thomas. 'Why?'

'It just slipped out one evening. I thought it would be harmless her knowing. She still had to prepare. I swear I had no idea about her taking Annabel's pitch until after everything happened,' replied Thomas, his eyes full of shame.

'So you just used me?' he asked, turning to Sandra.

'Oh relax. It's not like you didn't get something out of it,' replied Sandra.

'So this was all just so you could get revenge?' asked Annabel.

'I knew David would leave you sooner or later if you continued pursuing this dream of yours and taking the job away from you was just the cherry on the cake,' said Sandra grinning.

'Enough,' said Jonathan, raising his voice. 'There's nothing more I need to hear from either of you. Thomas and Sandra, collect your things and leave the building. You're both suspended until further investigation.'

Sandra didn't move.

'I'll call security if I have to, so please leave quietly while you can,' said Jonathan firmly.

Annabel sunk into a seat in Jonathan's office after Sandra and Thomas had left.

'I'm so sorry about this, Annabel. I swear I had no idea. I would have never given the job to her otherwise. I shouldn't have agreed to hire her in the first place. I'm such a fool.'

'You didn't know,' said Annabel. She sat there in silence for a while. She didn't know what to think anymore. 'I just can't believe it that someone would go to this extent,' said

Annabel staring into space. 'Am I okay to leave?' she asked after a while, feeling a headache coming on.

'Of course. Do you want me to call you a cab?'

'No, I'll be okay, I just need to digest all this.'

'Sure, take your time.'

As Annabel had stepped out onto the pavement, the noises around her grew fainter, her head throbbing. Her instincts told her something was wrong with how Sandra got promoted, but Annabel had been quick to dismiss it. Now it was all there in black and white in front of her.

Sandra was only hired because of Thomas in the first place and he also had a hand in her getting promoted. *I can't believe that David knew that Sandra got a job here. Why did he never say anything to me?* The thoughts, bounced around her skull like flashing sirens. *Oh my God. That's why she was so keen on changing the manuscript. She knew I loved it and seeing it being turned into this commercial garbage was killing me.* The intensity of Sandra's grudge against her shocked her.

She felt like standing on a ledge tilting forward, but not able to fall. Her earlier headache roared back to life, pounding harder as the pain spread across her forehead. The high-pitched sound in her ear grew louder and the drum of blood thumping at her temples created a symphony from hell.

She'd given Sandra the benefit of the doubt when Sandra told her this thing between her and Thomas had only been going on for a few weeks. *A bold-faced lie*. Annabel had convinced herself that Sandra got the job because she deserved it. She had even doubted herself and her abilities and thought she was not cut out to be an editor. *How could I have been so naïve to take her word? I should have trusted my instincts.*

She should have been angry at Sandra but instead, she was disappointed with herself. *I'm so stupid.*

The idyll of the last couple of days was a distant memory. She couldn't shake the thoughts that forced their way into her consciousness, despite knowing that they were the last thing she needed. She couldn't recall how she got to the station or onto the train, but the next thing she remembered was the announcement of her stop coming up.

By the time she got off the train, her headache was unbearable. Getting home and lying in a dark room was all she wanted to do but she wasn't sure that'd be enough to make it go away. The realisation that she used her last painkiller a few weeks earlier didn't help either. With no other option, she headed to the supermarket on the way home.

Ice patches formed on the pavement all around as the cold night drew in. Occupied with her thoughts, navigating the slippery path was challenging. After a few near misses, she quickened her steps in a desperate need to get away from the noise of the busy road. She marched on, narrowly avoiding bumping into a man standing by the shop entrance.

'Why don't you watch where you're going?' the man snapped at her.

'I'm sorry.'

Their encounter was brief, but there was something odd about the man's stance. She looked back. He was talking to a woman, his voice inaudible, but his hand gestures, his puffed out chest and the terrified look on the woman's face alarmed her.

Not one to interfere in other people's business, she made her way to the pharmacy section and picked up a box of painkillers with 'Forte' written on them in large red letters. As she headed to the checkout, she tried but failed to get the woman's expression out of her head.

Looking in the direction of the shop entrance, she hoped to spot them, but she couldn't see them from where she stood. *Don't be stupid, Annabel. It's not your place.* As people moved forward to the checkout, she suddenly remembered her task.

Stand up for what you believe in

She closed her eyes. This was the last thing she needed.

She was almost ready to abandon the queue and put the box back on the shelf when a shop assistant waved at her to come over. Her heart pounded in sync with the throbs of her headache at the thought of what she was about to do.

She paid and slid the box into her pocket, her hands trembling. When she stepped outside the man was still there, worked up, now shouting loudly at the woman. People passed by in a rush, desperate to avoid getting involved. Annabel wasn't one to interfere, but she felt compelled to say something in the woman's defence.

With her heart thumping loudly, she approached them. 'I'm sorry, but is this man harassing you?'

The woman stayed quiet, but her eyes spoke to her in a way Annabel couldn't explain.

'I don't mean to overstep. I just want to make sure you're okay.'

'I'm all right. Don't worry about me,' said the woman, after some hesitation.

'Who the hell are you?' the man shouted at Annabel. 'This is none of your damn business so stay out of it.' The man turned to the other woman, his back to Annabel.

'This is all your bloody fault. Embarrassing me in public again.' he shouted at her. 'Why do you always cause a problem?'

The woman flinched as he made a jerky movement.

As uncomfortable as she was feeling, Annabel knew she couldn't just walk away.

She stepped forward. 'I'm sorry, but you can't talk to her like that.'

'I told you to mind your own business. She's, my wife. I talk to her however the hell I want. Now get the hell out of my way.'

The man seemed to get more and more agitated. He grabbed his wife's arm and tried to move her away from the shop entrance.

'Get in the car,' he yelled at her.

'Sir,' said Annabel in a stern voice that took her by surprise. She stepped forward again and tapped him on the shoulder.

By this time, the man's irritation was palpable. He turned towards her, pushing his chest out even more. His behaviour reminded Annabel of an angry baboon. She hoped that he wouldn't have the nerve to physically attack her in public, but she couldn't be sure. He walked towards her, clearly trying to intimidate and force her into backing out of the situation.

Annabel stepped back a bit.

Without taking his eyes off her, he kept moving forward. As he took another step in her direction, he suddenly slipped on the ice, losing his balance and landing in front of Annabel.

Stunned, Annabel didn't quite know how to react. The man's wife hurried to his aid as he sat up clutching his knee. By this time a couple of patrolling police officers arrived at the scene. *Thank God they're here. Someone must have called them.* As soon as the officers set foot on the pavement, the man pointed at Annabel, accusing her of assaulting him.

She tried to explain to them that this was not what had happened, but with the man getting more and more agitated they decided it was best to take them all down to the station for further questioning. Cooperating was the best option and she had nothing to hide so she was more than willing to go along and clear everything up.

The ride to Twickenham Police Station wasn't a long one but sitting on the cold bench at the back of the van wasn't exactly comfortable.

The initial processing didn't take long once they arrived at the station. Just as the woman behind the desk confirmed the date and time, she suddenly remembered her interview the next day. Her stomach fizzing with nerves again, she tried to remain calm. *It will all be fine.* They took her details, and an officer took her phone, watch, boots and other possessions off her before she got escorted to a cell.

Annabel sat down on the bench as the large metal door clanged shut behind her. Spending time in a prison cell wasn't a bucket-list item she wanted to tick off, but somehow, she didn't panic. She felt at peace, knowing she didn't do anything wrong. It was all a misunderstanding that she hoped would be cleared up soon enough. She was more concerned about the other woman. Grateful that the officer had allowed her to take one of the painkillers before she was moved to the cell, her headache had slowly started to wane.

The barrenness of the cell was strangely calming, but without a watch or a clock she had no way of telling how much time had passed since she was brought to the station. It might have only been minutes, but as time went by Annabel grew increasingly anxious. *Why aren't they letting me go? Surely it shouldn't take so long to clear things up.* She didn't want to cause trouble and ask, but wished that someone would come and give her some information.

Finally, the cell door opened and a female officer appeared. Annabel hoped that she would be let go, but instead they took her to another room to take her statement. She explained everything as best as she could remember and told the officers that she was sure witnesses could confirm the same.

'We're gathering witness accounts and will speak to the other two people involved,' said the officer.

'I hate to ask, but do you have any idea how much longer that might take?' asked Annabel.

The officer reassured her that it probably wouldn't be too long, before she escorted Annabel back to the cell.

She tried to stay positive but grew increasingly concerned about her looming interview. Despite the angst, she was exhausted. Tossing and turning she tried to find a comfortable position. Lying on the bench, she couldn't see what was happening outside, but she could hear the sound of shouting as more people arrived at the station. *Their case was clearly more urgent*, thought Annabel as time passed without further news.

Even with the lack of comfort and the constant buzz of the bright neon light over her, Annabel managed to sleep for a while, only to be woken by a loud clang. It took her a few seconds to work out where she was and to realise that her cell door had opened once more. It was still dark outside, and she wasn't sure how long she had slept for. It felt like minutes, but it could have been hours.

'Miss Tate,' called out the female officer standing by the door. 'The charges against you have been dropped and you're free to go.'

At last. 'What time is it?' she asked as she followed her out of the cell. With still no shoes on, the ground felt cold against her feet.

'It's just past seven thirty in the morning,' replied the officer.

Relieved that she hadn't missed her interview, she was eager to get out of the station, but she still had some paperwork to go through.

'Do you mind if I make a quick call before I fill these out?' she asked.

'Of course. Go ahead.'

Although she still had some time, it wasn't enough for her to get home, get changed and head to her interview. She needed a plan quickly, so she dialled the most helpful person she knew.

'Hi Lucy,' said Annabel with relief as her friend answered the phone. 'I know it's school run time, but I'm in a bit of a situation. It's a long story, and I don't have much time to explain… but I'm at Twickenham Police Station. And before you ask, I'm fine.' She explained that she wouldn't have time to go back home before her interview at nine. 'I know it's a big ask, but could you pick up a couple of things from a shop and come down here to meet me? I just need to finish filling out some forms.'

'Oh my God. Erm… leave it with me. I'll get Hugh to drop the girls off this morning and I'll be there as soon as I can.'

'You're a star. I'll explain everything later.'

With all the paperwork completed, Annabel sat down waiting for Lucy when a woman approached her. She recognised her from outside the shop the night before.

'Hi. Do you remember me from yesterday?' she asked.

Annabel nodded.

'Just wanted to say how sorry I am about last night. I told the officers what happened,' she said. 'Rich can be a bit difficult at times. I'm really sorry you were caught in the middle. I know you were only trying to help, and I can't tell you how nice that was. I mean, I don't even know you. I don't think anyone's ever stood up for me like that before. Let alone a total stranger.'

'Thanks for clearing things up. I hope I didn't make things worse for you. That wasn't my intention at all, but I couldn't just walk by and do nothing.'

'Rich was pretty mad about it all, but I'm kind of glad you stepped in. I'm not sure where I go from here, but I'll figure something out.'

'I can't imagine how hard that must have been for you. But there's help out there.'

'I know. It won't be easy, but the officers were really helpful. They managed to find me something for tonight and I have an appointment with the council later to get something more permanent. But I don't want to keep you. I better go now. Thank you again.'

'I hope things work out for you,' said Annabel.

Just as the woman left, Lucy walked through the doors with a shopping bag and a cup of steaming hot coffee that Annabel could smell as soon as she approached.

'Thanks for coming.'

'I was so worried when you called. I brought the things you asked for and some breakfast. Do you have much time left?'

'I should be able to make it there. Still have about forty minutes or so,' said Annabel looking at the large wall clock hanging over the front desk. She took the bag from Lucy and headed to the toilets.

The tap was hard to turn, and it took a while before hot water dribbled out of it. She splashed her face with it a few times before wiping her hands and face on a coarse blue paper towel. She looked at her reflection in surprise; tears were streaming down her face. The pressure of the last twenty-four hours was too much to bear. She allowed the tears to roll down into the sink before she took a deep breath, splashed more water on her face and wiped it dry. She scrutinised the outfit she'd been wearing from the day before as she screwed the cap of the toothpaste back on and adjusted a few flyaway hairs. Her top was creased in many places and her snow boots and jeans weren't exactly sharp interview attire, but she could have done worse. *I should have asked Lucy to bring some clothes along. But at least I'm not wearing jogging bottoms.*

'I feel a lot better now,' she said as she emerged.

Lucy handed her the bagel and the coffee before sitting back down again.

'So, are you going to tell me what happened then?' she asked.

Annabel told Lucy what happened with Sandra and about the scene outside the shop the night before, and how she ended up at the station.

'Oh my God. This is mad. But I still don't understand why you got involved in this whole thing,' said Lucy.

Conscious of how her friend might react Annabel hesitated. 'Well, the note in the calendar said to stand up for what I believe in, so I kind of did.'

'Are you serious? This is all because of that stupid calendar?'

'Not exactly. I wanted to help her. She was clearly in distress. I couldn't just do nothing.'

'You could have called the police.'

Annabel had to agree that in hindsight that sounded like the right thing to do, and it would have been much easier. She wasn't sure why she didn't think of it at the time. 'It was instinct.'

'But you could've got hurt. If it wasn't for that stupid task none of this would have happened,' said Lucy, visibly upset. 'Maybe you should abandon the rest of the windows. At this rate, God knows where you could end up.'

'It wasn't the calendar's fault, Lucy. I made the decision, and no one forced me to do it. Please stop worrying. Besides, I only have five windows left. I'm hardly going to give up now. But I really need to get going, or I'm not going to make it on time,' said Annabel.

'Yeah, you better hurry up. Text me later and please call me before you decide to do anything drastic again,' said Lucy as they left the station.

Annabel tried to gather her thoughts on the way to the interview, going through the different questions they might ask her. She was nervous. She hadn't had time to prepare as she wanted to, and the revelation of Sandra's vendetta had really shaken her.

She kept going over the conversations she'd had with David about his ex-girlfriend. There weren't many and it was only when they'd first met. As hard as she tried, she couldn't recall anything that could have alerted her. She tried to remember if he'd mentioned her name, but nothing came to her mind about that either. She still had five minutes spare as she turned the corner of Harrow Road and she tried to redirect her thoughts to the task at hand. Reaching the building, she saw a discrete sign for Molière Publishing. She took a deep breath and pressed the bell on the intercom.

'I'm here to see Iona Lewis,' she said as the receptionist answered.

'Push the door.'

The foyer felt a lot less imposing than the one at Herold & Hains, but the interior was clean and modern. It almost felt strange not to hear the echo of her footsteps as she made her way to the reception desk.

'Could I take your name, please?' he asked.

'It's Annabel Tate.'

'Thank you. If you'd like to take a seat over there, I'll let Iona know you're here.'

With an audible inhale she walked over to the chairs next to the window. Her stomach was in knots, her hands clammy. Yesterday, her plan was to get a good night's sleep, wake up early and maybe even have time for a run. She had everything prepared. Her clean, ironed shirt and pencil skirt hung on the outside of her wardrobe. But the plan had changed.

As she looked down at her skinny jeans and snow boots, she felt unease about arriving in yesterday's clothes. But whether she liked it or not, there was nothing she could do about it.

As she tried to drown out the nagging voices in her head, a woman approached wearing a burgundy dress. She held her hand out to her and said, 'I'm Iona. You must be Annabel.'

'I am. Lovely to meet you.'

'Likewise. Shall we go?' she asked, leading Annabel towards the corridor.

Despite her initial nerves, Annabel felt the interview was going well. Iona was indeed a lovely woman and despite her shaky start, Annabel soon felt on familiar ground. Both Iona and Rachel, the other interviewer, seemed genuinely impressed with her level of understanding and involvement in her current position and were keen to tell her more about the company and the role. She could feel she was on the homestretch when Iona asked her, 'Have you ever been asked to do something at work that was against your core values? And if you have, how did you deal with that?'

Annabel's pulse quickened. Her thoughts raced in search of an appropriate answer, but all she could think of was keeping Sandra's secret.

'It's okay if nothing comes to mind,' said Iona, sensing Annabel's hesitation.

'Erm,' started Annabel clearing her throat. 'I'm not sure if this works as an example, but I've worked on a project recently where the project leader had decided to take a different direction from the original proposal based on a commercial argument. I felt that following on with that would end up ripping the essence of the work away.'

'So, what did you do?'

'Well, at first I tried to raise this with them, but they were adamant that the original proposal would not be commercially viable.'

'So, did you leave it at that?'

'No, I proposed that if I could show that the original idea was commercially viable, would they consider working with that concept.'

'And did they?'

'Initially, they said it would be too much work and we had a tight deadline, but then agreed to consider it.'

'What made them change their mind?'

Annabel could feel the blood rush into her cheeks. She couldn't exactly tell Iona that she essentially used her knowledge of Sandra's affair as leverage.

'I think I was probably annoyingly insistent,' she said finally.

'And did they end up running with the original plan?'

'No,' replied Annabel.

'And how did that make you feel?'

'Frustrated. Disappointed.'

'So, how did you reconcile this within yourself?'

She was conscious that she was taking a long time to answer, so she said the first thing that came to her mind. 'I haven't. It's kind of part of the reason why I'm here.'

'Thank you, Annabel,' said Iona with a smile. 'I just have one last question. How do you feel about working weekends?'

Annabel paused. A month ago, she would have said, yes without hesitation. But things have changed. She knew that showing flexibility and commitment to the role were huge bonus points in interviews, but where had that got her so far?

'Erm… I'd prefer not to work weekends. I'm looking for a role with a bit more work-life balance,' she said finally.

'That's great, thank you. Do you have any questions for us?' Iona asked as they finished.

'How soon would you need this person to start?'

'The sooner the better really but we'd be happy to wait a bit longer for the right person. What sort of notice are you on?'

'Seven weeks, but I might be able to negotiate it down to a month.'

'That's good to know.'

As they got to the end of the interview Iona told Annabel that they'd confirm the outcome to her in the next few days, before she went to see her out.

'It was lovely to meet you, Annabel,' said Rachel.

'You too,' Annabel replied as Iona walked her out the door.

Annabel stopped and turned to Iona.

'Is there anything else you wanted to ask?' Iona asked.

'No,' Annabel said, hesitating. 'But I wanted to apologise for my attire. I don't normally dress like this for interviews, but something happened last night and I wasn't able to go home.'

Annabel could have left it at that or made excuses, but she felt that she may have blown her chances already with her last couple of answers. Even if the truth sounded a bit far-fetched it was best to be honest, so she told Iona about her arrest and her eventual release, reassuring her that there were no charges made against her in the end.

'Thank you for telling me. It must have been a stressful night for you.'

Annabel watched Iona's face, searching for a clue as to what she thought of her confession. She couldn't tell if she was just being polite or if she genuinely didn't mind.

She walked up Harrow Road towards the station with a sick feeling in her stomach and thoughts swirling in her head. Did *I really tell them that I'd quit if things don't go my way?* She thought her answer showed impulsiveness, and her confession to Iona about her trip to the nick cemented her thought that her chances were slipping away. *They either thought I was raving mad or that I made the whole thing up.*

She hadn't realised before how much her body ached. As she moved from her train seat and stepped towards the door, she noticed a dull pain in her shoulders. *Can't wait to get into bed.* She stepped out of the carriage and set off in the direction of the high street, where people rushed about as usual, until she got to the vet practice. An ambulance was stationed outside, with one wheel mounting the curb. As she turned towards the entrance, a paramedic appeared wheeling someone out on a stretcher.

'Mrs Sharp,' she mumbled as she spotted the pale face.

Mr Ito followed them out of the practice, his expression a dark cloud.

'What happened?' asked Annabel.

'It's her heart, I think. I just hope she'll be all right.'

With Mr Ito busy talking to the paramedics, Annabel didn't want to get in the way, so she decided to head home. *I can come back later and check on him.*

'What a day Marley,' she said as she collapsed on her sofa after feeding him. Not wanting to think about her interview or about Sandra, David or her job at Herold & Hains, she dragged herself to the shower in the hope that the hot steam would soothe her aching body and make her feel better.

It was already lunchtime when she realised she hadn't opened her Advent calendar. The events of the last twenty-four hours should have been enough to put her off opening another window, but she was strangely excited about having a look.

Volunteer to help out

Annabel didn't need to think hard to come up with ideas to help people out. She was happy to lend a helping hand wherever she was needed, but more reluctant to ask for support when she needed it herself. Marley jumped up on her lap as she contemplated the options.

'What do you think, Marley? Who should I help out?'

He started to purr, rubbing his face against Annabel's hand.

'You want some attention, do you?' she asked as the purring became louder. She sat there for a few seconds, stroking him, when a thought occurred to her.

'Actually Marley, you gave me a great idea. I better head back down soon to see how Mr Ito's doing. But let's have some lunch first.'

Annabel entered the busy waiting room of the vet practice and sat down on one of the empty chairs. Despite his owner's best efforts, a rowdy Jack Russell kept barking at a cream-coloured Ragamuffin cat, looking rather indifferent lying in the safety of its pet carrier.

'Stop it, Teddy.'

Teddy didn't seem to pay much attention to his owner's request and continued yapping, only to be joined in the barking contest by a German Spitz. Annabel smiled politely at them. *The chaos could have certainly benefited from Mrs Sharp's military rigour*, thought Annabel as Mr Ito appeared from one of the treatment rooms with an English Bulldog and her owner.

'Apply the drops three times a day for the next week and it should take care of the problem, Mrs Campbell. If you don't see an improvement by next week, bring her back down.'

He scanned the room, clearly trying hard to remember who was supposed to be next.

'Come on through, Mr Williams.'

The man made his way to the treatment room with a pet rabbit. Just as Mr Ito was about to go in after them, he spotted Annabel.

'I'll just be a minute, Mr Williams.'

He walked up to her and asked. 'Is there a problem with Marley? I can't remember seeing your name on the list for today.'

'No, he's fine. I just came to see how you're doing.'

'That's very nice of you. I'm all right, just a bit worried about Mrs Sharp. They said they'd call me with an update later.'

'I'm sure she's in good hands. And how are you doing without her?'

'It's not ideal, but I'm managing. I just hope the agency can find me someone at such short notice. But I'm not sure what my chances are, especially before Christmas. I might just have to manage it for a few more days on my own.'

'This might not be what you had in mind, but I'd be happy to help out for the next couple of days if that would be of any use. I don't claim to have any experience managing patient appointments, but I'm not bad at organising and planning things. It's up to you, of course. It was only a thought.'

'That's so kind of you Annabel, but I wouldn't want to trouble you. Don't you have to work, anyway?'

'I wouldn't offer if it was any trouble and I have a few days off this week, so that's not an issue. Just let me know and I can be on hand to help.'

'Thank you. I really appreciate your offer.' After a moment's hesitation, he said, 'A day or two's help would be fantastic. Just until I find someone a bit longer term.'

'No problem. I can start tomorrow. Let me know what time you want me here for.'

'We open at nine, so maybe if you could come in at eight, I could show you around on the booking system. But I better go now and see to Mr Williams and Hugo.'

'Of course. I'll see you tomorrow.'

Chapter 9

Annabel couldn't quite believe the whirlwind of the last couple of days. The strange scenes flashing in her memory seemed distant, like something out of a movie. She didn't want to think about the interview and the mess she'd probably made of it, so she looked forward to helping out at the vet practice later. She didn't want any drama. *An ordinary day would do me nicely.* With these thoughts, she approached the calendar on the table. She was a little hesitant to open the hatch behind number twenty-one but took a deep breath and thought, *it can only get better.*

Have a dinner party

That isn't so bad, she thought. But she'd had a busy day at the practice, and she was no Nigella in the kitchen, either. Her place looked tidy and presentable, so at least that wasn't an issue. After some consideration she thought she'd look up some recipes whilst on her lunchbreak and get the supplies after she finished her shift. All she had to do for now was to invite the guests. *Maybe I could ask Liv if she wants to come along*. But she didn't want to think about work or feel awkward about her recent interview. So, she quickly dismissed the thought. Instead, she rang Lucy to see if her and Hugh wanted to come along and thought she might ask Mr Adler as well. Lucy's parents were in town, so after a quick call and with babysitting taken care of, two of her dinner guests were confirmed. Mr Adler was next on her list, so she headed down the corridor.

'What a nice surprise,' he said. 'Those ginger biscuits you brought along the other day were lovely. I've finished them all.'

'I'm glad you enjoyed them.'

'Would you like to come in?'

'Maybe another time. I'm on my way to work. I've invited a couple of friends over for dinner and I was wondering if you fancied joining.'

'How nice of you to ask. It'd be lovely, but I don't want to intrude.'

'You wouldn't intrude. It'd be lovely if you could come.'

'All right then. You twisted my arm.'

'Dinner should be ready at seven thirty so come around then.'

As she made her way to the stairs, Annabel passed James's door. Hesitating for a moment, she turned back and knocked. She waited for a while and knocked again, but when no answer came, so she headed off to work.

The practice was busy all day. They had a couple of Border Terriers booked in for their jabs in the morning, and a French Bulldog for some dental work, and Annabel had taken a call from a lady with a poorly Poodle. She managed to squeeze her in just after one. Her day-to-day work at the publishing house couldn't have been more different. It was hectic at times, but that's where the comparisons stopped. Although she loved her job, the procession of meetings one after the other could sometimes feel monotonous. It felt refreshing to do something completely different and spending her day working with animals gave her great enjoyment even if it meant cleaning up after a rabbit with a dodgy tummy.

Once the initial flurry of patients had eased, Annabel decided to take her lunch and plan her evening menu. Trying different cuisines was right up her street, and although she often read the recipes in her supermarket food magazine with great enthusiasm, she had to admit that didn't really amount to much practical experience. Eventually she came across a chicken curry recipe. Reading through the list of ingredients she could almost smell and taste it. *How difficult could it be*? One thing she was confident about was a tried-and-tested chocolate and ginger cake recipe that never failed to impress. It was one of her mother's favourites, and she wasn't easy to please. Just as she'd worked out her shopping list, the lady with the poorly Poodle arrived. Mr Ito was on time, so she showed them into the treatment room. He soon found out that Layla had an ear infection, and they were sent on their way with a couple of days' worth of antibiotics.

24 Windows

It was after four o'clock when the last patient left the practice.

'I don't think we have any more bookings for today, do we?' Mr Ito asked.

'No, Mrs Newman was the last one for today.'

'Thought so. You can get off now if you want. I can manage it for the next hour or two.'

'Are you sure?'

'Yes. And I can't thank you enough for helping out today. I don't know what I'd have done without you.'

'Don't mention it, Mr Ito. I'm really happy I could help. How's Mrs Sharp doing? Have you heard from the hospital?'

'She's doing a lot better. I think they're keeping her in for a couple more days for observation. Just to make sure she's all right, then they'll probably let her go home for Christmas.'

'That's so good to hear.'

'She won't be back until the new year, but the agency has found someone to fill in for her between the holidays.'

'That's great news. What time do you want me to come in tomorrow?'

'Eight thirty should be early enough. I won't need you all day. The practice is only open until two, so you can get off earlier.'

'No problem. I'll be here nice and early.'

Mr Ito was about head back to his office when Annabel asked, 'Do you have any plans for this evening?'

With Mr Ito confirmed, Annabel's guest list was almost complete. Just as she finished her shopping for the dinner party an idea came to her. A conversation she had with Mr Ito earlier made her think. She still had some time spare, so she decided to visit the local animal shelter a few streets away. Walking past the enclosures, she didn't know exactly what she was looking for, but soon she stopped in front of one of the cages. The kennel's resident pounced around happily without a care in the world. Annabel recognised the breed. It was a little silver Scottish Fold no more than seven or eight weeks old. The rescue centre manager who showed her around said she had been found abandoned a couple of days ago.

'She didn't have a collar or a chip, so it would have been hard to find out anything more about her. She's so funny. She thinks she's a little tiger. I'm sure it won't be long before she finds a new home,' said the shelter manager.

Annabel stood there for a moment looking at the silver kitten.

'She's a beauty, isn't she? I think I'd like to take her, but I'll need to have a think first,' said Annabel.

'Of course, that's understandable. Come back when you've decided. But I can't guarantee she'll still be here. We'll also need to do a home visit before we can release her.'

'That's fine,' she said, glancing at her watch with a start. 'I'll let you know, but I've got to go now.'

It was just after five o'clock by the time she laid out all the ingredients in the kitchen. Realising she hadn't spoken to James yet, she headed over to number twenty-four and knocked.

As the door opened Annabel forgot to breathe for a moment.

'Sorry… erm, is this a bad time?' she asked, as James pulled a t-shirt over his wet hair.

'No, just came back from a run. Haven't seen you out there lately. Have you given up already?'

'I've not given up,' said Annabel in a slightly sulky tone. 'Just been a bit busy, that's all. Anyway, I came over to ask if you wanted to come over for dinner tonight. I've invited a couple of friends and wondered if you'd like to join. Came around earlier to ask, but I don't think you were in.'

'Sounds great. What time?'

'Around seven thirty should be fine.'

'Do you want me to bring anything?'

Annabel thought for a moment. 'A couple of chairs, if you don't mind.'

He raised an eyebrow. 'Chairs?'

'Yes. There will be six of us and I've only got four chairs.'

'Oh, I see. Sure, I'll bring a couple around.'

The cake mixture was ready to go in the oven and her curry was bubbling away. With things seemingly under control, her thoughts turned to her guests for the evening. She'd known them for varying lengths of time, but in the last few weeks they had all played an increasingly important role in her life. Their personal stories and their often level-headed advice had made Annabel think about her life on more than one occasion and she was grateful for their gentle and often unintentional guidance as she navigated the last few weeks. Just as she had put some rice on the boil and started to set the table, the doorbell rang. It was only seven o'clock when Lucy and Hugh arrived.

'Something smells nice. Thought we'd come early to see if you needed a hand with anything,' said Lucy.

'That's nice of you, but I've got everything under control. I think. You just help yourself to a drink,' said Annabel. 'And before you ask, I'll tell you later about the interview, just not tonight.'

'Of course. I won't ask a thing.'

Just as Annabel had taken the cake out of the oven and put it aside to cool, the doorbell rang again.

'Could you get that for me, Lucy? I think it'll be Mr Adler.'

The elderly man stood there, clutching a box of chocolates. Impeccably dressed as always, he'd even donned a red dicky bow for the occasion.

'It's lovely to see you again, Mr Adler,' said Lucy. 'Come on in.'

'Oh, have we met before, dear? I'm sorry, but my memory is not as it used to be.'

'Don't worry. We only met briefly the other day. Me and the girls helped Annabel bake the gingerbread biscuits.'

'That's right. I remember now. They were delicious.'

Lucy escorted him into the living room and introduced him to Hugh. They chatted for a while when the intercom buzzer went off. Annabel went to answer it.

'Come on in, Mr Ito.'

He was carrying a bottle of wine and a small bag of Marley's favourite treats. The last one to arrive was James. Annabel opened the door to find him stood by a couple of chairs holding a bottle of wine.

'Come on in,' said Annabel. 'Thanks for bringing the chairs.'

They carried them in, and she introduced him to the group. Annabel took the bottle from him.

'I hope you like it. It's one of my favourites,' said James.

Annabel turned the bottle around to look at the label and she couldn't believe her eyes. She wasn't a big wine connoisseur and there were only a couple of wines she liked, but this German Riesling was one of her favourites, too.

'It's not everyone's cup of tea, but I think it's quite nice,' said James.

Everyone seemed to be getting along and having a good time.

'I hope you're all hungry,' said Annabel as she brought the food in. The aroma of the spices filled the room as everyone took their seats around the table.

'You can help yourselves,' she said, before heading back to the kitchen to check on the cake and move it from the cooling rack. She could hear the clinking of cutlery as they tucked in. Annabel was still out of sight when James broke the silence.

'Is it just me, or this curry is really hot?' he said.

'I'm so glad you said that,' replied Hugh. 'I didn't want to sound like a whimp, but I feel like my mouth is on fire,' he continued as Annabel came into the room.

'Is there something wrong with the food?' she asked.

'I think you might have gone a bit overboard on the chilli, Annabel,' said Lucy. 'What recipe did you use?'

'Just one off the internet. It said to put two green chillies in. They didn't have any green ones at the shop, so I got some red ones instead. These ones here,' she said, holding up a small, wrinkly looking pepper.

'Those are Scotch Bonnet chillies, Annabel,' said Lucy. 'No wonder the food is so hot.'

'Maybe I should have brought some milk instead of the wine,' said James with a smile.

'Very funny,' said Annabel, not even attempting to mask her sarcasm.

Lucy suggested diluting the mixture with coconut milk and after a few minutes the heat level of the curry was brought down to safer levels. Despite the initial hitch, they all liked the food, and everyone seemed to be having a good time. To top off the night, Annabel's cake was a triumph. They managed to avoid the topic of work for the most part, and Mr Ito told everyone how much of a help Annabel had been at his vet practice.

'A woman of many talents,' said James.

'Indeed. I don't know what I'd have done without her,' said Mr Ito.

'You would have been just fine, I'm sure of that,' said Annabel with a smile.

The conversation turned to their Christmas plans. Mr Adler was invited to his sister's house in Kent, along with his son and his family.

'When are they arriving?' asked Annabel.

'On Christmas Eve.'

Mr Ito had plans to spend Christmas Day with his niece in London, Lucy and Hugh had a jam-packed day lined up with the girls, and James was leaving for Scotland to spend the holidays with his family up there.

Mr Ito and Mr Adler left soon after they finished the dessert, and James carried some plates to the kitchen, helping Annabel tidy up.

'Is everything all right?' he asked. 'You've been a bit quiet at times.'

'Yes, it's all good. Just had a bit of a tiring week.'

'I thought you took some time off work?'

'I did, but things just went a bit haywire,' said Annabel, as Lucy walked in.

'Oh, you've told James about the arrest?'

Annabel stopped breathing for a second, her feet rooted to the ground and with her eyes fixed on Lucy. She thought she could get through the whole evening without the arrest or her ordeal with Sandra coming up.

'What arrest?' asked James.

'Oh my God. I'm so sorry,' said Lucy. 'I just thought that's what you've been talking about.'

Annabel gave James a brief summary of the events that had led to her night in the cell.

'You were lucky you didn't get hurt. Maybe I should keep an eye on you just to make sure you don't get into any more trouble,' said James.

'You know, that wouldn't be a bad idea,' said Lucy smiling.

'Very funny, but I can look after myself,' said Annabel.

'Dinner was lovely, and that cake is to die for. You've got to send me the recipe,' said Lucy to Annabel as she said goodbye to her in the kitchen a while later.

Annabel had to agree. The food had turned out quite well – despite her inability to identify searingly hot chillies – but thankfully they all managed to leave with their tastebuds more or less intact.

'And the coconut milk saved the day. It was a great idea,' said Annabel.

'I'm really sorry for bringing up the arrest earlier. I just thought that's what you were telling James,' said Lucy.

'Don't worry about it. It was all good in the end.'

'Still. I shouldn't have said anything. But James seems nice,' said Lucy.

'Yeah, he's a good neighbour to have around.'

'Just as a neighbour?' probed Lucy.

'And a friend of course.'

'Nothing more?'

'What are you getting at, Lucy?' asked Annabel, her tone slightly defensive.

'I was only asking. There's no need to get all funny about it.'

'I'd better get going as well,' said James, appearing at the kitchen door. 'Thanks for dinner.'

Annabel felt a bit frazzled, wondering if he'd heard their conversation. 'Thanks for coming along and bringing the chairs. And the wine. I hope it made up for the missed dinner a few weeks ago,' she smiled.

'I think we're quids in now,' said James, smiling.

***

The next morning Annabel was still riding high on the success of the previous night. It had been a long time since she'd had guests over and she'd really enjoyed herself. She was getting ready for work when her thoughts turned to the kitten, she saw the day before. After their discussions last night, she grew increasingly more confident that her plan was the right one. Feeling excited, she rushed down to the shelter before her shift to arrange a home visit for later that day. The manager was on duty when she arrived and once Annabel took another look at the boisterous kitten, her confidence grew that she was making the right decision.

'Thanks again for inviting me over yesterday. It was good to spend the night in such great company,' said Mr Ito, when she arrived at his practice.

'I'm glad you had a good time. Have you heard anything more about Mrs Sharp?'

'Not yet. I might give the hospital a call later. I think her daughter has been in to see her every day.'

'I can give them a call later if you'd like and check to see how she's doing.'

'That'd be great. Who do we have in first thing?'

'Ms Hays with Maya I think, but let me check.'

'Oh yes. I'll get the jabs ready for her.'

The practice was a lot calmer than the day before and the last patient left just after two.

'That was the last one on the list for today,' said Annabel.

'That's great. I think I can manage it from here with the odd drop in. You go home early.'

'Are you sure? I can stay a bit longer if you need me.'

'No, you head off. And thank you ever so much for all your help. I'm really grateful.'

'Don't mention it. I enjoyed doing something different.'

Annabel wished Mr Ito a lovely Christmas and rushed home to meet the manager from the shelter. The visit didn't take long, and the manager was satisfied that the kitten would be happy in her new home. They headed back to the shelter to complete the necessary paperwork, and Annabel was soon on her way home with the kitten in tow.

When they arrived back home, Annabel opened the box to let her out. She was inquisitive, and although Marley was being more tolerant than usual, after a short while he seemed to get annoyed at her playful jabs.

'Don't worry, Marley, she's not staying with us for long. But be nice to her for the time being.'

When Annabel finally sat down for a cup of tea, she should have been feeling content, but something didn't feel quite right. She recounted her morning at the practice and her visit to the shelter and quickly checked through the paperwork again to make sure she had everything in order. It wasn't long before she realised what was amiss. With all the excitement, she had completely forgotten about the Advent calendar. Not wanting to waste any more time, she opened the window and read the scroll.

Book a holiday

Annabel couldn't remember the last time she took a proper holiday. Her and David had planned to go to the coast a couple of times but work always got in the way. Memories of a vacation abroad were even fainter ones. She took the odd day here and there to run errands and visit her family, but the thought of not going to work for two weeks somehow terrified her. Every day was a chance to achieve her goal and every day she wasn't there could have been a missed opportunity. If someone had told her a month ago to book a holiday, she'd have resisted it with all her might, but with everything that happened lately she was past caring. She even felt she deserved a break.

There was just one problem. She had no idea where she wanted to go. These things usually took careful planning and having to make a decision so quickly made her slightly nervous. *I came this far*, she thought. *I'm not going to give up now.*

Having a plan always made her feel better, more in control. So she took out a large map from behind the wardrobe. She laid it on the dining table and dusted off the frame. She had meant to put it up on the wall, but it was one of those things she never got around to doing. After looking at it for a while and seeing she wasn't getting anywhere, she decided a more drastic approach was needed. She closed her eyes, took a deep breath and jabbed her finger at a point on the map.

'Please don't let it be the North Pole,' she said.

Peeking through her fingers, she realised it wasn't. But she was pointing at a place in the middle of the Pacific Ocean. Slightly disappointed, she closed her eyes once more.

'Let's try again.'

The second jab landed in the Caribbean Sea. It was a bit closer to land this time, but it still didn't pinpoint an exact travel destination. After inspecting the group of islands lying to the right of her index finger, a moment of disappointment was followed by relief. It might have been a common bucket list item to enjoy the winter sun for a few weeks on a Caribbean Island, scuba diving and swimming with pigs in the Bahamas, but Annabel couldn't justify travelling that far just to complete her challenge. The environmental impact of her trip aside, she had to admit that her complexion wasn't exactly suited to temperatures above twenty-five degrees either. Even with constant application of factor fifty, she often found parts of her skin crozzled in a matter of minutes. The thought of suffering from jet lag for days on end made the trip even less appealing.

'Dry land would be good this time,' she said, as she placed her finger on the map for the third time. She opened her eyes, and to her delight, her fingertip was on land. Although she could tell it was in Italy, it was more difficult to make out the exact location. On closer inspection, and after a quick check on the internet, she managed to make out the name.

'Verona,' she exclaimed triumphantly. 'This is much better.'

With a European travel destination, she didn't have to worry about crossing many time zones, and having a choice of transport options besides flying made her feel even better. Keen to avoid getting on a plane, she started to research travel options from London. It didn't take her long to come across a website advertising train journeys on the Orient Express departing from London Victoria. Her excitement was slightly dampened when she saw the price of the ticket. She had a fair bit of money saved up in rainy day funds that she never touched, but somehow, she didn't feel a holiday on a historic train amounted to a rainy day.

After more research on hotels in the area, she found a cheaper deal on a holiday booking site. Still not sure if she could commit to doing something so out of her comfort zone, she decided to take a break and come back to the task later.

She had planned to take the kitten down to the vet practice after dinner, but the thought of leaving her there alone for the whole night somehow didn't feel right. *It could be stressful for her, being there alone in the dark in a strange place for so long. Better if I take her early in the morning*. She was happy she could enjoy the kitten's company a little longer, even if Marley decided to sulk at not being the centre of attention for a day.

Time went by quickly and Annabel was intent on going to bed early so she could get up before Mr Ito arrived at the practice. With her guest settled in the bedroom and Marley guarding his spot on the bed, she was just about to turn the lights out when she suddenly remembered that her task for the day was still incomplete.

She turned her computer back on, clicked through the bookmarked pages and scrutinised the options once more. Looking through them for the second time filled her with even more excitement. She could picture herself on the train taking in the views on the way to Verona and admiring the sights as she walked across the city. If it wasn't for the hefty price tag or the fact that she had less than two hours to make a decision, she wouldn't have hesitated, but ingrained habits of overthinking were difficult to shake. *Maybe I could go for something a bit less extravagant. Like taking the Eurostar to Paris.* The alternative option was still an appealing one, but despite the huge price difference it still didn't feel right. Annoyed that the clock was ticking and she still hadn't made her decision, she pushed the computer to one side and went to the kitchen.

'Maybe I need a sign,' she said as she lifted a mug out of the cupboard. Perhaps if it was fate telling her to take the trip, she could have justified the price. Staring at the cup as she dunked a bag of camomile tea, she wasn't sure exactly what sign she was waiting for. She turned on the radio and a travel program came on.

Her mouth dropped open when she heard the host discussing iconic train journeys around the world. His guests talked about the epic journey on the Trans-Mongolian Railway crossing six time zones, and the iconic Canadian Railway through the Rockies with steep inclines and tracks winding through thick forests, breath-taking mountain views and stunning waterfalls.

'That could be it.' Annabel had asked for a sign, and as much as she chose not to live her life by chasing good omens, she couldn't help but wonder if this was one she should act on. The many adventures depicted in books always sounded magical and reading about them created a safe distance from the complexities they brought, but those adventures weren't hers. Thoughts zoomed around in her head as she contemplated the events of the last few weeks. She could continue living her life the way she had done, keeping a safe distance from the drama and unpredictability that taking risks brings, or she could go on her own adventure. The choice was hers.

The impulsiveness of the decision took her by surprise as she went straight back to her computer and booked a ticket to Verona on the Orient Express.

Filled with excitement, it took a while before Annabel fell asleep. And about halfway through the night, the kitten decided she wanted to join her and Marley on the bed. She found it difficult to jump up, so she meowed until she was finally lifted up amongst them. When her alarm went off at half past five, Annabel wasn't ready to wake. The first cup of coffee helped her somewhat, but it was a slow start.

She got dressed and gathered everything together before scooping up the kitten and putting her in the pet carrier she'd borrowed from the practice the day before. Armed with some cat food, cat litter and a couple of bowls, she headed out. She was walking along the corridor just as James's door opened.

'Oh my God. You scared me.' she said, stepping back a bit. 'What are you doing awake at this time?'

'I'm heading for a run. What are you doing up so early? I don't think the vet practice is open at this time,' he said gesturing at the box in Annabel's hand.

'Oh… I know.'

Thinking that Annabel might be about to do something that could get her into trouble he asked, 'What are you up to now? Please tell me it's not another one of those calendar tasks.'

'I'm just returning something I forgot the other day,' said Annabel sheepishly.

'Let me take a look,' said James, crouching down to the box.

'You took a kitten?'

'Shhh, no. All right… if you must know, I'm taking her as a surprise for Mr Ito.'

'Does he know?'

'It's a surprise, so no, he doesn't. But I'm sure he will like it.'

'Are you sure?'

'Well, I think.'

'You think? I mean it's not your usual fruit cake sort of surprise… take it or leave it.'

'Argh… I just think he really needs this. Anyway, I have to go. You enjoy your run,' said Annabel, setting off towards the stairs.

'No way. I'm not letting you go there on your own. God knows what kind of trouble you'll end up in.'

'I don't need a chaperone, thank you very much. I can deal with this myself.'

'I'm sure you can, but I'm still going with you.'

'Fine, but just please keep quiet,' said Annabel, as they set off.

By the time they had got to the practice it was nearing quarter past six. Mr Ito liked to start early so there wasn't much time to waste. She hadn't returned the keys after her last shift the other day, so getting in was easy; but she knew that getting into Mr Ito's office was going to be a bit more of a challenge. She instinctively turned on the torch on her phone.

James put his hand over the light. 'I don't think that's a good idea,' her whispered.

'You're right. It would probably be more suspicious than having the lights on,' she said, flicking the switch. She checked the office door just in case, but it was locked. Annabel was never given a key to it, so she started looking around the room. She suddenly remembered seeing a key safe in one of the cupboards at reception. She was certain Mrs Sharp had a copy for emergencies. When she opened the box, everything was labelled meticulously.

'Good old Mrs Sharp'.

She turned the lights out and, armed with the key, she opened the door. The room was dark, but she could make out the outlines of the furniture. Everything was left neat and tidy, just how Mr Ito liked it. Annabel and James walked in and, closing the door behind them, she headed to the large pet cage in the corner of the room. She put a tray of cat litter in the far end and a bowl of food and water in the other. She placed a blanket on the floor and put Tora's toy on it. At last, she opened the pet carrier and let the kitten venture into her night hide.

'Come on, Tora. It's safe to come out.'

She took a bit of convincing, but soon she was sniffing around the cage.

'I promise you won't have to stay here on your own for long.'

She closed the cage door as the cat continued to meow.

'We're not going just yet. Don't worry.'

Annabel sat down at Mr Ito's desk and turned on the lamp. She looked around for a piece of paper and pen and started to write.

Dear Mr Ito,

I hope you'll forgive me for sneaking into your office. I've met this little girl and I couldn't help but think that what you and she needed was the same thing: a companion to share life with. This might be a long shot, but I know how much you miss Kitaro and that no one could ever take his place. That's not what this is meant to be.

At six weeks, she already has bags of personality, and I thought the name Tora would suit her. You'll soon see why. She's looking for a true companion who's willing to look after her and I hope she might have found it in you.
I know taking her in would be a big commitment and I hope I haven't overstepped. But I can understand if you can't.
Her and Marley have made friends already, so I'm sure he wouldn't mind her being around if you don't think the time is right.

Merry Christmas,
Annabel

When she finished, she folded the piece of paper and placed it on top of the cage.

'Come on Annabel, we better get going,' said James.

'Bye, Tora. Be a good girl,' said Annabel.

Annabel had put everything back in its place and locked the door to the practice. They'd started to walk up the street and just in the nick of time as she noticed Mr Ito walking along the opposite pavement towards the building. James ducked into the next side alley and grabbed Annabel's hand, pulling her alongside him.

'That was close,' she said, still holding on to James's hand.

'I told you it's better if I come along,' he smiled, his face inches away from hers.

Annabel felt her pulse quicken. Conscious that James might notice too, she pulled her hand away. 'I think we can go now,' she said, peering out onto the street.

It didn't take them long to get home and Annabel was full of excitement.

'Do you want to come in for a coffee?' she asked when they got up the stairs.

'Sure,' replied James, glancing at his watch.

'I just need to wait now,' said Annabel as she sat down on the sofa, coffee in her hand, anxiously checking her phone.

'I'm sure he'll notice soon enough, and he'll be in touch,' said James. But with every passing minute, Annabel grew more and more concerned that her idea might have been a step too far. The anticipation of an angry phone call or a text was becoming too much to bear.

'God, what must he be thinking?' She began to pace up and down the room. Her phone buzzed as a text came through. Her heart beating fast, she opened it with a lump in her throat.

Thank you, Annabel, and Merry Christmas from me and Tora. P.S. Mrs Sharp said 'thank you' for the lovely flowers. She said they brightened up her room.

Annabel jumped to hug James in relief.

'Good news then,' he said as Annabel had let go of him.

'Sorry, just feel so relieved that he's not angry.'

'Thank you again,' said Annabel as James headed for the door. 'And I'm sorry you missed your run.'

'This was way more exciting. Plus I managed to keep you out of trouble,' said James smiling. He was about to leave, but turned back. 'Do you want to get some food this evening? If you're not busy. Just before we both head off for Christmas.'

Annabel didn't reply straight away.

'Not like a date. Just two friends,' said James, sensing her hesitation.

'Sure, that'd be nice.'

'Great. How about if I cook this time?'

'Oh.'

'Don't look so surprised. Like you said, I'm a man of many talents,' said James with a smile, regaining his usual composure.

'I'm beginning to see,' said Annabel, returning his smile.

'Shall we say eight then?

'Sounds good.'

Annabel closed the door behind her. Confused at first, she wasn't quite sure what had happened. Was this a date? James said just as friends, and she was clear she didn't want a relationship after everything that had happened over the last month. Why was she feeling so odd about the whole thing, then? And what was that earlier in the alley? *It was probably nothing*, she thought, as her thoughts turned to the Advent calendar on her dining table. Only two windows remained shut on it. She contemplated what they might hold and whether her secret benefactor had saved something special for the last couple of days as she opened the hatch.

Orsolya Kiss-Toth

Make a change

Annabel could think of many ways she could make a change. Some ways were more impactful than others. She had been contemplating switching to a new brand of coffee lately, but she didn't think that would be much of a challenge. But confident she could come up with something more meaningful, she carried on with her day. She looked forward to going back to the jewellery shop after breakfast to see the finished pendant for her sister. She wondered if it would be like the one Abi had lost all those years ago.

She entered the shop accompanied by a familiar jingle and headed towards the till. She hadn't noticed it last time, but in the far corner of the shop a collection of old vinyl lay in a box perched on a mahogany dresser. Arlena was still at the back, so she started to browse through the contents while she waited. A couple of faded covers from the 80s reminded Annabel of the sounds of her childhood. *Rick Astley. Mum used to love listening to this one. I wonder if their old record player still works.* She pulled the record out of the pile and put it to the side before she continued flicking through the others. Just before she got to the last one, she stopped on a light blue cover. She took it out of the box and turned it around. Sliding the vinyl out of its cardboard sleeve, she checked it before slipping it back in.

'Have you found anything you like in there, my dear?' came Arlena's voice.

'Yes. I'll take these two,' said Annabel, approaching the till.

'He was a handsome young man,' said Arlena, gesturing at the cover. 'Here's your pendant.'

Annabel took the shiny jewel into her hand, running her fingers across the rays of the sun.

'It's beautiful. I can't believe how much it looks like the one my sister had.'

'I'm glad it's close enough.'

'It's better than close enough. It's almost identical.'

'Would you like me to wrap it up for you?'

'Yes, that would be lovely.'

Arlena took out a small padded green box and placed the pendant in the middle before tying a ribbon around it.

'Here you go.'

She paid and wished Arlena a Merry Christmas before she headed back out into the cold. Leaving the quirky little shop with Abi's Christmas gift in her pocket and the wrapped-up vinyl in her hand, Annabel felt excited about the days ahead. A month ago, the thought of spending Christmas with her family would have been the most preposterous idea anyone could have ever suggested to her, but now she started to look forward to it. Humming a Christmas song, she headed back to her flat.

No sooner than she put the vinyl on the table, her phone rang.

'Hello.'

'Hi Annabel, it's Iona calling from Molière Publishing.'

'Oh, hi Iona. What a nice surprise. I didn't expect your call so soon.'

'I didn't want to keep you waiting for too long.'

'I appreciate it,' said Annabel. *It probably wasn't a difficult one after that massive blunder.*

'So, I was wondering, how would you feel about visiting our office in Paris towards the end of next month?'

Annabel's voice faltered. 'Erm… I didn't realise there would be a second round of interviews. And abroad, too.'

'Oh, no. We'd like to offer you the role if you're interested. If you accept, part of the induction would be in the head office in Paris.'

Annabel was speechless. She was certain she'd blown her chances. She had rehearsed her gracious loser response many times, but she didn't prepare for this.

'Annabel, are you still there?'

'I am. Sorry. It's just taken me by surprise. I wasn't expecting… I mean, after I told you about my night at the police station, I didn't think you would… Sorry. I'm not making much sense, am I?'

'Don't apologise. Your honesty was refreshing, and I think you've got a real eye for literary talent. But you still haven't answered. The job is yours if you're still interested.'

Over the last couple of days, Annabel hadn't allowed herself to think about what getting this role would mean to her. Searching her mind, she was more confident than ever that this was the job she wanted. Her heart beating fast, she recalled her Advent challenge for the day. *Make a change.* But would she just be running away from her problems at Herold & Hains if she accepted? Realising that this was all she'd ever wanted, she took a deep breath before she answered.

'I'd love to accept it,' she exclaimed.

As her answer came, she felt certain that she wasn't running away from anything. She was running towards the dream she'd held for many years. She didn't answer without fear of what this change would bring, but she was ready to embrace the new challenge.

Annabel was giddy with excitement as she packed her bag for the Christmas holidays. She couldn't believe Iona had offered her the role and that her dream was to become a reality. The years of hard work, late nights and all the sacrifices were worth it in the end. She couldn't wait to tell James. She wanted to call her mother and tell her – shout it from the rooftops – but this also meant the end of a significant chapter in her life.

It had just gone twelve when an email arrived from Iona with her contract attached. This was the last confirmation she needed that her dream was actually becoming reality. After all her packing was sorted and the presents were neatly wrapped, she sat down at her dining table in front of the computer. She sat in silence for a while before she started to type. Fifteen minutes of bursts of taps on the keyboard was followed by pauses and the repeated thumping of the backspace key before she was finished. She read the lines on the screen and typed up an email to Jonathan. With the letter attached, she was ready to hit send. She hovered over the send button for a moment, considering the weight of her decision. Once the email was sent, there was no going back. But she didn't want to go back. She was ready to face a new challenge. Just as she was about to commit to her decision, a text flashed up from Jonathan.

Hope you're okay, Annabel. There's no rush but let me know when you have some time to talk. Once things have settled a bit, I'd like to discuss your role with you.

Annabel hesitated before she replied. Contemplating her options, she checked her watch. She still had time to go to the office. *Maybe it's better if I do this in person*, she thought as she changed the recipient of the email and replied to the text.

I can be in the office in an hour, if that works?

With a meeting agreed, Annabel got ready to head into the city.

Only a couple of people lingered in the office when Annabel got there. She turned on her computer and sent a document to print before knocking on the door of Jonathan's office.

'Come on in,' sounded Jonathan's voice. 'Thank you for coming to the office, Annabel. Hope I didn't trouble you too much.'

'No, I was going to come in anyway,' she said, taking a seat.

'I just wanted to let you know that both Sandra and Thomas have left Herold & Hains. I won't go into the details, and you'll be aware of quite a lot already, but there was plenty of evidence that showed that Sandra obtained her role at Herold & Hains and later the promotion through unethical means. And that she plagiarised your pitch, too. I'm really sorry that this wasn't picked up earlier and that things got this far.'

'I appreciate that,' said Annabel, not surprised by any of what Jonathan said.

'You've been a valuable asset to this company ever since you started and I should have done this a long time ago, and I'm really sorry for that. But I'd like to offer you the editor role as well as a generous raise and an increase in the level of your company benefits. I've also added a bonus to that based on the work you've done over the last couple of years. It was well overdue.'

'Wow, thank you,' said Annabel, taken aback as Jonathan passed a job offer letter to her stating her new title and the increase. The raise was almost double her current salary and still a significant increase to the one offered by Molière Publishing. The words on the paper in front of her were all she'd ever dreamed of: for her skills to be recognised and rewarded. But it didn't feel like how she had envisaged it. Not after everything that had happened.

'So, I hope you accept the offer and can start the role in the new year.'

Annabel hesitated. It would be so much easier to just stay and then all her hard work would have really paid off, but it didn't feel right. 'I'm sorry, but I can't,' she said finally.

'Oh. Is it the salary? I can speak to my boss about that.'

'No, it's not that. I… I really appreciate it, but I came to give you this,' she said, handing over her resignation letter to Jonathan.

Jonathan slumped in his chair. 'Is there anything I could do to change your mind?'

'I don't think so,' said Annabel after some thought. 'I just think it's time I moved on.'

They sat chatting for a while and Annabel told Jonathan about the new role she had been offered. He was very pleased for her, but sad it had got to this point.

'You'll be great,' he said as he led Annabel out of his office. 'And you know that the door is always open here.'

'Thank you and Merry Christmas,' said Annabel before she left. Her thoughts slowly settled as she made her way home.

With a wrapped-up present and a box of chocolates, she headed down the corridor to say goodbye to Mr Adler before she left for the holidays.

'I hope I'm not troubling you,' she said as he opened the door.

'No, not at all. It's always good to see you. Come on in.'

'Just wanted to wish you a lovely Christmas before I head off to Masham tomorrow. Your family arrive in the morning, don't they?'

'Yes, Charlie messaged me earlier. They're on the last flight now.'

'I bet you can't wait to see them. I brought you a little something that I hope you'll enjoy,' she said handing him the wrapped package.

'You shouldn't have bothered. I hope it's nothing too fancy.'

'It's only a little something. Don't worry.'

'Do you mind if I open it now?'

'Of course not. Go ahead.'

As he undid the wrapping paper, the cover of a record was revealed. He stroked it gently and a tear pooled in the corner of his eye.

'I hope I didn't upset you,' said Annabel quickly.

'Not at all. It's a very thoughtful gift. Thank you. Would you like to have a listen?'

She smiled and nodded.

Audrey Hepburn's sweet voice filled the room. Annabel enjoyed the music and appreciated it, but she was sure that the memories it evoked for Mr Adler were more than just an appreciation of great music. It was of a life well lived and a companion sorely missed.

'She had such a beautiful voice,' said Mr Adler when the music stopped. They sat chatting for a little while before Annabel stood up.

'I'd better get going. Still have a few things to pack for tomorrow. You have a lovely time with your family, and I'll see you when I'm back,' she said, hugging him.

'Thank you. You enjoy your Christmas too, won't you?'

Mr Adler insisted on seeing Annabel out, but his steps seemed a bit slower than usual and his breathing a bit more laboured.

'Are you feeling okay? I hope I didn't upset you with the music,' said Annabel as she turned to say goodbye. 'You're looking a bit pale.' She noticed earlier that he didn't seem his usual self, but she thought maybe it was just a bit of tiredness and the anticipation of seeing his family. Now she wasn't sure if that was all.

'Not as fit as I once was, but I'm all right. Don't you worry about me.'

'As long as you're sure. Knock on my door if you need anything at all tonight. I'll be around until midday tomorrow.'

Just when she finished her sentence his face contorted and he reached for his chest.

'Mr Adler. I think you better sit down.'

Annabel tried to hide her panic, not wanting to alarm her elderly neighbour as she led him back to the couch.

'I'm sure it's just a bit of indigestion. Had a big meal earlier. That must be the culprit.'

'I'll get you some water and stay for a bit longer.'

'There's no need for that. You go and get on with your things.'

'Only ten minutes. If you look better after that, I'll go.'

After a few sips of water, he seemed to be in better spirits, but the colour still hadn't returned to his face and a hint of perspiration appeared over his brows.

'Your hands are stone cold,' said Annabel as she took the glass from him.

'That's quite normal at my age, dear.' He laughed weakly, then suddenly clutched at his chest again.

'That's it. I think it's best if I call the doctor, and please don't protest.' Annabel took her phone out of her pocket and dialled.

'I don't want to waste their time. I'm sure it's nothing serious.'

'You're not wasting anyone's time. I'd be much happier if they checked you out.'

He stopped persisting after a while and Annabel went to the hall to stay out of earshot. She feared the worst but didn't want to worry him too much. The operator reassured her that someone was on the way and they'd be with her in the next ten minutes or so. She sat back down on the sofa, fidgeting and checking the time on her phone every minute.

The intercom buzzer rang. *Finally*. Relieved, Annabel let them in. She waited at the door to speak to one of the paramedics before they entered the room.

'I'm so glad you're here. He's inside on the sofa. He insists that he's fine, but he complained about chest pain, and he doesn't look too good.'

'Don't worry, sweetheart. He's in good hands,' said one of the paramedics. Annabel showed them in. Seeing that Mr Adler was in safe hands, she slipped out to her apartment to get her coat and collect a few things just in case before returning.

Mr Adler was still adamant he was fine and that all the palaver was completely unnecessary, but they managed to convince him that it'd be best to go to the hospital to get him checked out. They sat him in a wheelchair and put an oxygen mask over his mouth and nose, getting ready to take him downstairs.

'Do you mind if I go with him?' asked Annabel turning to one of the paramedics.

'Are you a relative of his?'

'He's my neighbour. His son and his family are flying in from Australia tomorrow. He lives alone.'

'It should be fine as long as he's happy with you coming along.'

'I'm sure he won't mind but I'll ask him.'

As they started their descent on the stairs, Mr Adler gestured to Annabel.

'Would you mind getting my little phone book off the dresser? It has Charlie's number in.'

'Of course, I'll go and grab it.'

With the keys in her hand, Annabel rushed back to the flat, taking the stairs two at a time. When she'd almost reached Mr Adler's apartment, James's door opened.

'What's going on?' he asked.

'Oh, God. I completely forgot about dinner,' said Annabel, turning to him. 'I'm really sorry, but I can't make it. It's Mr Adler. They're taking him to the hospital to get him checked out. I'm going with him.'

'Don't worry about dinner. What's happened?'

'He's been having some chest pains.'

'Which hospital are you going to?'

'I'm not sure, but I need to get something for him. I better hurry. I don't want to hold them up.'

James followed them down and went straight to the driver.

'Which hospital are you taking him to?' he asked.

'St George's.'

'Thanks. I'll go after you in a bit,' he said to Annabel as she got into the ambulance.

The calm professionalism of the paramedics was a stark contrast to Annabel's state of mind. She tried her hardest to suppress the slightest signs of worry, but her eyes gave her away.

24 Windows

'Everything will be all right,' sounded Mr Adler's voice from behind the oxygen mask, muffled by the shriek of the siren. She managed a faint smile as she reached for his hand. He seemed frail and his skin even paler in the glow of the bright neon lights of the ambulance. His paper-thin skin barely covering the dark web of veins running across his hand. *He has to be all right.*

'You'd better wait here,' said a paramedic to Annabel as they wheeled Mr Adler through to an examination room.

'You did the right thing calling us. And don't worry, he's in good hands now. They'll keep you updated.'

A few people sat around in the waiting area and Annabel made her way to one of the white chairs. The cold plastic creaked as she settled in. A few rows behind her a man sat with a dressing pressed against his forehead, only the corners of the cloth looking remotely white. Occasionally he let out a couple of moans and groans as the alcohol started to wear off. She didn't want to judge, but the injury seemed self-inflicted. Opposite sat a woman with a young boy, his arm in a homemade sling. He didn't make a sound, but the ever-so-faint lines on his cheeks told Annabel he must be in pain. The room was quiet for the most part, apart from when the paramedics wheeled in a woman on a stretcher, her head held in a neck brace. Her injuries were clearly a priority, as they whisked her away along one of the long neon-lit corridors.

Nervously fidgeting in her seat, Annabel kept checking the large wall clock. It had only been thirty minutes since they arrived, but for her it seemed like hours.

Then unexpectedly, James walked through the door. He quickly scanned the room before making his way to her.

'Have they said anything yet?' he asked.

'No. They're probably still running some tests.'

'So, what happened?'

Annabel told James everything.

'You did the right thing. It's best to get him checked out.'

Annabel searched his face. It was different. His eyes couldn't hide his concern. She wanted him to tell her that everything was going to be fine, but at the same time she felt drawn to his vulnerability. They sat in silence.

The hours passed. The young boy left with a sparkling white cast and the man's head wound had been stitched up before he was let go on his merry way. Soon it was only Annabel and James sat in the deserted room.

Finally, one of the doors opened and a young woman approached them, wearing a long white coat over her light blue scrubs.

The woman walked up to her. 'Are you Annabel?'

Annabel nodded.

'I'm Dr Khurram. I've been overseeing Mr Adler's care.'

'How is he?' she asked eagerly.

'He's doing better. We ran a few tests and managed to rule out a heart attack,' the doctor said, her voice calm.

'That's good,' said Annabel, relieved.

'Have you managed to find out what caused him to be unwell?' asked James.

'Yes. It took a while, but it seems he's got an infection. We've started giving him some IV antibiotics and some fluids to address the dehydration. He's responding well to that. You were right to persist that he came in.'

'Could we go see him?' asked Annabel.

'We're still arranging a bed for him on one of the wards, but you can go in now if you like.'

They followed Dr Khurram to the examination room. Mr Adler lay on the bed with the drip above his head and the heart monitor beeping along steadily next to him. His face lit up as he saw them come in.

'You're still here? You should have gone home. I told you that everything will be all right. And what is young James doing here?' he asked with a faint smile.

'Just came to see you were looked after,' said James.

'The doctor told me they're keeping me in for the night. I told them it's not necessary, but she's very insistent.'

'Yes, she said they're just sorting out a bed for you on the ward. I haven't rung Charlie yet, but I'll let him know where you are so they can come here,' said Annabel.

'Just tell him not to worry. He can panic a bit. Got that from his mother.'

'Don't worry, I'll tell him.'

'Thank you. But after that, please go home.'

'Not yet. I'll wait for you to be taken upstairs first. But you go,' said Annabel, turning to James. 'I'll be all right.'

'I'm staying. And please don't even start to tell me otherwise.'

It took a couple of more hours before the ward was ready to receive him.

'Your bed is ready now, Mr Adler,' said Dr Khurram as she entered the room with a nurse.

Annabel asked James to get the details of where they were taking their elderly neighbour before she slipped out of the room. Opening Mr Adler's little phonebook, she quickly scanned through the names. Charlie's was one of the first ones on the list. She dialled the number. It went straight to voicemail. *They probably haven't landed yet*, she thought as she checked her watch. *I'll try him again in a bit.*

A text flashed up from David. Annabel's heart skipped a beat as she opened it.

I just heard what happened. Are you okay? It would be good to talk x

'I don't have the energy for this,' she mumbled as she closed the text. Just as she was about to put her phone away, another text pinged up.

'Seriously?' she exclaimed, but soon felt relieved when she saw it was from James with directions to the room. She followed the signs up to the sixth floor, spotting James waiting just outside of the nurses' station.

'Did you manage to speak to Charlie?'

'Not yet. His phone is still turned off. I'll try him again a bit later. I know I said that I'd leave once they brought him up, but I don't want to go until I've had a chance to speak to Charlie. You don't have to stay, though. I'll be fine.'

'I told you. If you're staying, I'm staying as well.'

'Aren't you heading up to Scotland today?' asked Annabel.

'I am, but my train doesn't leave for another eight hours. I've already packed, and I can get some sleep on the train, so I can stay for a bit longer.'

'But don't feel like you have to. Honestly, I'd be fine on my own.'

'I know you would be, but I'm sticking around. I'm going to get a cup of coffee. Do you want one?'

'That'd be nice.'

James made his way down to the café on the fifth floor and Annabel tried calling Charlie again. This time the line rang out, and finally he answered.

After a short introduction, Annabel told him what happened with his dad and reassured him that he was doing well.

'We're in St George's. If you come up to the sixth floor and ask at the nurses' station, they'll direct you to his room.'

'Thanks. I'll get Ruth and the kids over to the flat and then I'll come straight to the hospital. I shouldn't be too long.'

It wasn't long before James returned with two cups of steaming hot coffee. 'Here you go. Coffee. Milk, no sugar if I remembered right. I brought these separate, in case,' he said as he handed her the cup and two sachets.

'Well remembered. And no sugar, thanks. Spoke to Charlie whilst you were downstairs. He's on his way.'

'Great. Do you want to wait for him?'

'Do you mind? I don't think he'll be too long.'

'Of course.'

It was just after five in the morning when Charlie arrived. Annabel recognised him straight away. In the flesh, she could see the unmistakable resemblance between father and son: their mannerisms alike, and the same steel blue eyes looked back at her. But his suntanned skin was a stark contrast to his father's pale complexion, and his blond hair provided a reminder of what his father looked like before the soft greys took over.

'Charlie?' she said as she approached him at the nurses' station.

'Hi. It's Annabel, isn't it?'

'Yes, we spoke earlier. And this is James.'

'Hi. How is he?'

'He's asleep at the moment, but I think the antibiotics and fluids are helping. The doctor didn't seem too concerned when they brought him up.'

'That's a good sign, I suppose. I was so worried when you called. It really concerns me, him living by himself. I tried to persuade him to come out with us or even to move closer to Margot, my aunt up in Kent, but he's so stubborn.'

'Yes, he mentioned it. He seems happy here, though, and we look out for him.'

'That's really good of you. I can't thank you enough for bringing him in.'

'Don't mention it. He wasn't easy to convince, but we got here in the end.'

'It wouldn't be him if he didn't insist on people not making a fuss around him,' smiled Charlie.

'That's Dr Khurram,' said Annabel as she approached.

She introduced them before they made their way to Mr Adler's room. Dr Khurram checked the drips that were nearly finished and asked one of the nurses to swap them for new ones soon. Happy that his temperature had gone down, and his vitals were normal, she reassured Charlie that his dad was on the mend.

'Will he need to stay another night?' he asked.

'I'm not sure at this point. If he keeps improving as he has done, we might be able to let him go in the morning on Christmas Day.'

When the doctor left, Annabel went to say goodbye to Charlie.

'We'd better get going now, if you don't mind,' she said.

'Of course. It must have been a long night for you both. And thank you again. I'm really grateful that you've been here with him.'

Just as they were about to head off, Mr Adler opened his eyes.

'Are you still here?' he asked, looking at Annabel.

'We're going now, but Charlie's here.'

'Charlie. So good to see you, my boy!'

'We'll leave you to rest, Mr Adler. And I hope you're out of here by Christmas morning,' she said with a smile. 'Merry Christmas.'

'Thank you, Annabel.' He smiled. 'And Merry Christmas to you both.'

Charlie promised to keep them updated and said he might see them after Christmas, as they planned to stay for a few weeks.

'What a night,' said Annabel as her and James got into the taxi.

'It certainly was eventful.'

'I'm sorry about dinner.'

'Don't be silly. We can have dinner another time. It's really good of you to look out for him like that. He's lucky to have you around,' said James, a soft smile around his lips as he reached over to put his hand on Annabel's.

Annabel's heart beat faster as she readied herself to say something, but the moment seemed to have passed when he pulled his hand away. Emotions mixed in her head from the events of the night; she was too tired to think. She turned to gaze at the empty streets as they passed by.

Chapter 10

Shattered after the long night at the hospital, Annabel collapsed on the sofa. As much as she wanted to stay awake, her body surrendered to the slumber. She only woke when the phone rang.

'Hello?'

'You sound a bit groggy. Did I wake you?' asked Lucy.

'What time is it?'

'It's ten thirty. Just wanted to know what time you'll be dropping Marley off. The girls are so excited to have him stay.'

'Oh my God. I didn't realise the time. I should be getting ready. I'll be at yours around half twelve. My train leaves at two.'

'Are you okay, Annabel?'

'I'm fine. Just had a bit of a night.'

'You didn't get arrested again, did you?'

'Very funny. Nothing like that. I'll tell you when I get there.'

'Thank God.'

'I better get going now. I'll see you soon.'

She put the phone down and headed to the Advent calendar, feeling a wisp of disappointment when she looked at the last closed window. As much as she dreaded some of the tasks, they had been life affirming. With no more windows left, she had come to the end of her journey. She carefully opened the last window, taking out the scroll.

Face your fear

Before she had time to contemplate the task, the intercom buzzer went off.

'Who's that?' she asked.

'It's me,' sounded David's voice.

What? I don't have time for this now. 'What do you want, David?'

'I just wanted to see that you were okay. You didn't reply to my text.'

'It's not a great time. I'm in a rush.'

'I won't take too much of your time, I promise.'

'Fine, come up. But I need to get going soon.'

'Hey.' He greeted her with a big smile and a kiss on the cheek, pressing a bouquet of flowers into her hands.'

'What's this for?' Annabel asked, closing the door behind him.

'I'm really sorry,' he said. 'I just heard what happened with… Sandra… and I feel awful.'

Marley followed David into the living room from a safe distance.

'Why did you never say that she came to work there?' Annabel asked, her eyes firmly fixed on David.

'I didn't want to make things awkward, and she said she'd leave.'

'But she didn't, and you knew it. You knew how I felt about her.'

'I know. And I'm really sorry. But I had no idea she would go to this length. I promise'

'You never said that you'd just broken up with someone when we'd met,' said Annabel. 'Why?'

'Because we hadn't. We broke up six months before that, but Lex – sorry, Sandra kept texting me. I told her it was over, and we had nothing more to discuss and eventually the texts stopped so I thought she got the message.'

'So how did she find out where I worked?'

'I don't know. Maybe a common friend told her. It wasn't me; I swear.'

Annabel wasn't sure whether to believe David or not, and she needed to get ready. 'Look, thanks for coming over and telling me this, but I really need to get going. I've got a train to catch.'

'Can I give you a lift to the station?'

Annabel hesitated. 'I'd really love if we could chat a bit more,' said David.

'Fine, but I need to get a shower. I'll be ready in fifteen minutes.'

'Great, I'll wait here.'

When Annabel emerged from the shower, David was sitting on her couch. 'I thought I heard a knock. Was someone at the door?' she asked.

'It was one of your neighbours. He left that,' said David, pointing at the bottle of German Riesling on the table.

'James,' she said, smiling. Picking up the bottle, she remembered her task. There were many things she naturally avoided. She feared that her lack of career progression had defined the lack of success in her life, and that without that she didn't know who she was. Having an honest conversation with her mother about how her words and actions made her feel over the years had seemed impossible. And her self-worth had been brought into question time and time again, with every setback another confirmation that she wasn't good enough. These anxieties had plagued her for years, and yet over the last few weeks she'd managed to start on a path to resolve them. They hadn't left her completely, but she'd taken steps to acknowledge their presence and impact and had started addressing them one by one.

Then a realisation struck her, and she suddenly knew what terrified her the most. It wasn't the new challenges of her career or the work ahead to rebuild her relationships.

She knew what she had to do. But could she? The what ifs were quick to appear in her thoughts, drifting through like thunderclouds across a blue sky. She knew that the longer she left it, the more excuses she'd come up with.

'James,' she said again. She rushed past David into the bedroom, pulling on a pair of jeans and a top.

'What's going on?' David asked.

Barely hearing him, Annabel gathered all her courage and walked down the hallway to number twenty-four. She knocked on the door with her heart pounding like it wanted to escape her chest. She didn't really have time to figure out what she wanted to say, but maybe it was best this way. *Just rip off the plaster.* She knocked again, but no one answered. She looked at her watch and realised that James must have left already for Scotland. Still high on adrenalin, she went back to her flat to find David standing there, confused.

'I need to go, David. Thanks for the offer of the lift, but I think I'll be fine.'

'When can we chat, then?'

'I don't know. I'm not sure I have anything left to say.'

'But…'

'Goodbye, David' said Annabel, opening the door.

After David left, she sat on the sofa for a while debating whether she should call James or not. She didn't have much time before she had to leave as well, so she got the last things ready and headed to the station.

Traffic seemed quieter than usual and there weren't many people about. Half an hour later she was at Lucy's house. The girls were excited to see Marley and after sniffing around the living room, he seemed to settle.

'Tell me, then. What happened last night?' asked Lucy.

Annabel didn't need much convincing, and she soon told Lucy about the previous day's events.

'Wow! That's amazing about the job. I'm so happy for you. And thank goodness you were around. I can't imagine what would have happened to Mr Adler if you didn't call for the ambulance.'

'It was just luck. But it was nice to have James there,' said Annabel.

'James, huh? That's nice of him to go with you.'

'Yes. It was, wasn't it?' said Annabel, glancing again at her phone. No messages. No notifications.

'I'm sure they'd have called you if anything changed with Mr Adler,' said Lucy.

'Pardon?'

'You've been looking at your phone for the past thirty minutes. I thought you were waiting for a call from the hospital.'

'From the hospital? Oh, no. I just need to make a call that I've been putting off.'

'You better get to it, then.'

She dialled the number, but there was no answer.

'I can't leave a voicemail,' she said.

'Who are you calling?'

Annabel passed her the scroll.

'I see,' said Lucy with a grin. 'I'm glad you can finally see it.'

'Was it that obvious?

'It was only a matter of time before you realised how you felt about him.'

'You knew? Why didn't you say something?'

'I tried the other day, but you went all defensive about it. I thought it was best to leave it. You were going to see it eventually, anyway. It was only a matter of time.'

'Oh, God. But now I don't know why he's not picking up. He came around earlier when I was in the shower, and he left a bottle of wine with David.'

'David? What was he doing there?'

'He texted me yesterday when I was at the hospital. He wanted to talk. I didn't reply so he decided to just turn up at my place.'

'And what did he say to James?'

'I have no idea. He just left the wine and now he's not picking up. I can't leave a voicemail. What would I even say? "Hey, I just realised that I like you and I think you like me too, how about a drink when you're back?" That's just lame.'

'Just keep trying. He'll pick up eventually. And don't worry about the task. If you can't speak to him today, you can do it when you see him again. But I've been meaning to tell you something since that morning at the station after your release. I just hope you're not going to hate me too much.'

'I know, Lucy,' said Annabel.

'What do you know?'

'About the Advent calendar,' smiled Annabel.

'Since when?'

'Since that morning at the station. Well, I didn't know, but I could feel that something wasn't quite right. And when I showed you the last task, you weren't surprised at all.'

'So, are you mad at me for meddling?'

Annabel stayed quiet for a moment. 'Of course not. If it wasn't for you, I would have still been doing the same job and probably would have never found out about Sandra. And I wouldn't have had the guts to pick up the phone to Becca or to sort my issues out with Mum. So, I'm not mad at you. I'm super grateful that you meddled,' said Annabel, laughing.

***

Christmas morning came with a fresh covering of snow. The scene from Annabel's bedroom window reminded her of a snow globe.

She had two messages waiting when she turned her phone on: one from Lucy and one from Charlie letting her know that Mr Adler was well enough to leave the hospital that morning. Even though he was allowed home, they thought it was best not to travel up to Kent because of the snow and his health, and had decided to celebrate Christmas at the flat just the five of them.

Annabel was delighted he was feeling better. Despite the great news, she was disappointed that there weren't any other messages. She needed a distraction to help take her mind off things, so she got dressed and headed down to the kitchen.

Abi and Hunter arrived just after breakfast and the girls helped Evelyn in the kitchen whilst Hunter kept George company in the lounge and Howler out of their way. After a lot of peeling and chopping amongst the chattering, Christmas lunch was almost ready.

'I'm so pleased for you, Annabel,' said Evelyn as she hugged her daughter. 'It's such an exciting adventure and you've worked so hard to get there. I can't wait to tell Ethel at the bookshop.'

Annabel felt uncomfortable with all the spotlight on her, but for once she was the centre of attention for the right reasons. Evelyn was proud of Annabel. She took a moment to process how this felt, a warm glow emanating through her chest. Even after she told them about her night at the nick, her mum couldn't have praised her more.

'You must be excited about going to Paris, and your trip to Verona sounds amazing. Now I wish we planned something like that for our honeymoon instead of two weeks lying on a beach,' said Abi.

'I'm sure you'll have a great time in Crete, too. I thought you had some day trips and sightseeing planned,' said Annabel.

'We have. But still, it's not the same. Your trip sounds so romantic.'

'Going alone isn't very romantic,' said Annabel.

'You never know. Maybe you'll meet someone on your trip,' said Abi with a smile.

Lunch was served in the dining room and Annabel could tell Evelyn was pleased to have all her family there around the table. The pop of the crackers was followed by groans at the painfully unfunny Christmas jokes before they all tucked in. The turkey skin looked crisp and the meat juicy and the roast potatoes golden. Evelyn had even made Yorkshire puddings – George insisted on having them every year.

'Your mother makes the best Yorkshires. I could eat them every day,' said George.

'It probably wouldn't be too good for your waistline, George,' said Evelyn.

After lunch they gathered in the front room to hand out the presents. Abi was struggling to hold back her tears as she unwrapped the box, revealing the pendant.

'This is so beautiful, Annabel. And it looks just like the one from Grandma. Where did you find it?'

'This woman near my flat makes the most beautiful silver jewellery and she made it based on the one I had.'

'That's amazing. You couldn't tell it wasn't the same one, Abi,' said Evelyn.

Amongst other things, her mother got Annabel a limited edition of The Velveteen Rabbit, a childhood favourite that she'd often requested her mother read to her, and the first book she read by herself.

'That's beautiful. Thank you, Mum.'

'I found your Bonnie in a box the other day. I remember how you insisted keeping her.'

'I still remember you carrying that stuffed rabbit everywhere with you,' said Abi. 'I thought she'd make it all the way to uni.' Abi laughed.

'I can't believe you haven't given her away,' said Annabel.

'How could I? It meant so much to you. Maybe you could take her back to London with you when you go,' smiled Evelyn.

George was happy with his scotch whisky and a new set of tools he couldn't wait to try out, and Evelyn was taken by feelings of nostalgia as they listened to Rick Astley. Howler didn't seem fussed about his new lead. He seemed most interested in rummaging through the discarded wrapping paper.

The weather looked bright outside and they decided to go for a walk after lunch to make room for dessert later. Howler was wary of the snow at first, but he soon got excited, running around and rolling in the white powder.

'What have we got for dessert?' asked Annabel.

'Your mother made Christmas puddings. Your Grandma's recipe,' said George.

Annabel's eyes lit up. 'Really? Haven't had Christmas pudding in years. The shop-bought ones are never as good as Grandma's. I don't even bother trying them anymore.'

'I haven't tasted them yet, so let's hope they turned out well,' said Evelyn.

'Maybe we could pick a few sprigs of holly for decoration,' suggested Abi.

When they got in, Evelyn put the kettle on for some tea and plated the puddings on a couple of silver trays. With a dusting of icing sugar and a sprig of holly each, they were ready to be taken to the table alongside a couple of jugs of brandy sauce.

'They look great, Mum,' said Annabel. 'I can't wait to try it.'

'Almost forgot,' said Evelyn. 'I've put a little something in the batter so just watch out for it.'

With excitement they tucked in and after quickly polishing his piece off, George was keen for seconds.

'How can you eat so quickly, Dad? I've hardly started mine,' said Annabel.

'I think he's after the hidden treasure Evelyn mentioned earlier,' said Hunter, laughing.

Just as he said the words, Annabel stopped chewing and pulled a shiny coin out from her mouth. 'I think I've found it,' she said.

'Lucky you. I suppose the search is over then, Mum. Unless you've hidden two of them,' said Abi.

'There was only one in the batter, I'm afraid. I just divided it between two moulds. So, no. There's no more to find.'

Abi and Hunter left in the evening and with the kitchen in order, Evelyn and George decided to go up to bed shortly after. Annabel sat by the fire in the living room with Howler laid by her feet, her book on her lap as she gazed into the flames, mesmerised by their glowing dance. Images of the ups and downs of the last few weeks came to her mind, her thoughts turning to the adventure that lay ahead. She hadn't thought about the significance of the changes she had started to create in her life over the last month. The connections she had made and repaired, her change of mindset. Even when she thought about her new role, she didn't think of it anymore as a goal to reach, but as a significant turning point in her life's journey. She remembered the words she had written on the Christmas wish card – *I wish I could find my path to happiness* – and although she knew Lucy had sent her the present that turned her life upside down, she couldn't help but feel there was something magical about that Advent calendar.

For a brief moment, she considered how things could have turned out if it wasn't for the festive gift, but she quickly dismissed the thought. She no longer had a place in her mind for what ifs. After all, this Christmas was one of the best she had had in years. The questions she tried to drown out in her mind no longer scared her. She felt content, but something – or rather some*one* – was missing. Amongst all the successes, she still felt a whisper of disappointment when she thought about not being able to finish her last challenge, but she didn't want to think about that now. It was for another day. She'd done all she could do, and she just wanted to enjoy being present.

***

After a few relaxing days over Christmas, Annabel had time to reflect a bit more and she felt recharged by the time she headed back to the city in the new year. Returning to Herold & Hains was a strange feeling. People were sad to see her go.

'I have no doubt in my mind that you'll do really well in your new role, Annabel. You'll be a real asset to them,' Jonathan said. 'I just wish there was something I could have done to make you stay. But I know what a great opportunity this is for you.'

He agreed that she could work only four weeks of her notice on the condition that she did a thorough handover. She found out from Jonathan that Mr Shaw decided to take his manuscript to another publisher, but he wasn't sure where. Annabel wondered if they would see the same potential in that she did. Beyond that, she still had a few projects to wrap up and she was happy to hand things over to Liv for her to take on more responsibility.

'I'll miss you, Annabel.'

'I'll miss you too, Liv. But it's not like I'm moving to another country. We can still meet up.'

'I know, but it won't be the same here without you.'

After work, Annabel headed over to Lucy's to pick Marley up and to have a chat.

'I hope he wasn't too much trouble.'

'Not at all, but the girls got really attached to him over the last couple of weeks. They'll be sad to see him leave.'

'They can come over any time to visit, you know.'

'Be careful what you wish for. They'll move in before you know it,' said Lucy with a laugh. 'You haven't told me yet. How was your Christmas? Did you have a good time?'

'I know you'll say "I told you so", but I did. It was really lovely to get away from London for a while and spend some time with them. It was exactly what I needed. Mum was over the moon about my promotion, and we talked a lot about my plans for the trip to Verona.'

'So, does this mean that you're not mad at me for making you spend Christmas with them?' asked Lucy.

'No. Quite the opposite, actually. You were right. I really needed to sort things out with Mum. All this unspoken stuff was just bubbling away under the surface, spoiling everything. I'm just so glad we can finally move on.'

'I'm pleased it worked out. Did you get a chance to speak to James since?'

'No. I've tried, but his phone has been off ever since. I think he was back for a couple of days after Christmas, but he was gone again by the time I got back. Mr Adler said he popped in to see him. I think he said he went away for work for a few weeks.'

'That's a shame. I'm sure you'll get to speak to him soon enough, though. And don't dwell on not being able to complete the last task. I know what you're like.'

'You know me too well. I'm not going to lie. I was a bit disappointed I didn't get to speak to him, but I'm sure I'll get the chance soon enough.'

'Exactly. And how's Mr Adler?'

'He's doing well. Recovered from his illness now and you could really see his mood lift with Charlie and the family around. I think they managed to visit his sister in Kent for new year too. He also told me that Charlie and the family have decided to relocate back to the UK in May. They had been thinking about it for a while now and his company offered him a role in London, so he decided to take it.'

'I bet he was over the moon about that.'

'Yes, it'll be good for him to have them nearby.'

***

The next few weeks went by quickly. Annabel felt strange knowing she wouldn't be there to see the outcome of the projects she had worked on, but gradually she handed over all her work to Liv. When the news spread across the company that she was leaving, emails started to come in telling her how much she'd be missed. Bit by bit, she said goodbye to everyone she had worked with over the years.

It felt strange when she arrived in the office on her last day. She'd thought she would be more emotional thinking about the end of such an important part of her life, but she found herself more excited about the future than anything else.

She didn't expect a huge send off, so it took her by surprise when people started to gather around her desk and a large cake was wheeled in just after eleven.

Jonathan said a few kind words about how much of an integral part of the team Annabel had been over the last seven years and how much she would be missed. He wished her well and handed her a card, a bunch of flowers, and a present from everyone in the team. Jonathan had always been good to her, and Annabel knew how much he appreciated the work she had put in over the years, but this was the first time she felt that her dedication was acknowledged by them all.

She fumbled her way through a short thank you speech and enjoyed a slice of cake with everyone around.

'I'm happy for you to leave early,' said Jonathan. 'Knowing you, I'm sure that by now everything is wrapped up.'

'Thank you. I've only got a couple of emails to send, and I should be done after that.'

'I have to go to a meeting now, so I probably won't see you before you go. Good luck again and keep in touch.'

Half an hour later Annabel shut her computer down for the last time, her desk tidy with no visible sign that she had ever been there.

'That's me done, Liv. I'm going to get going,' she said.

'Thanks for everything, Annabel. I hope your first day goes well next week.'

'I'll tell you all about it when I next see you.'

'Let me know when you're back from Paris and we can catch up. I'm sure you'll have loads of stories to tell.'

'Definitely.'

They hugged before Annabel gathered up everything and headed downstairs.

Joe was sat behind the desk at reception when she reached the foyer. 'An early finish today, Miss Tate. It makes a change,' said Joe with a smile.

'Yes, Joe. For the last time.'

'You take care of yourself and all the best,' he said.

'Thank you, Joe. You look after yourself, too.'

Pushing the large glass door open, she left Herold & Hains for the last time. Life was good and she was determined to make the most of it.

***

Annabel's first week in her new role went well. She met most of the team in the London office and got off to a good start learning about the work alongside them. She was keen to get stuck in and was certain that it wouldn't be long before she was trusted with a project of her own.

The next book club event was coming up, but with her trip approaching Annabel couldn't make it. She promised Lucy she'd come for the next one, but she was glad she had another month before she had to face Alex again. On Sunday she packed the last few items ready for her trip to Paris and got Marley's things ready to take over to Mr Adler's later. He'd offered to look after him for a week whilst Annabel was away. She didn't want to inconvenience him, but he'd insisted.

'He's such great company. You'd really be doing me a favour,' he'd said.

Annabel wasn't sure that was strictly true. She didn't consider it a favour to give anyone the job of cleaning out cat litter, but she'd gratefully accepted his offer.

'I hope he won't be too much trouble, but if you have any problem at all, please ring Lucy. Here's her number. She's happy to take him off your hands if it gets too much,' said Annabel.

'Thank you, but I don't think it will be necessary. We'll be just fine. Won't we, old boy? You have a great time, and we'll see you when you're back.'

Her week in Paris was a great experience. At the induction, she met colleagues from other European offices and some great locals who took her under their wing. Two fellow editors, Eleonore and Gabriel, showed her around the city, and she learnt a lot from them about the work at Molière Publishing.

With every passing day, she grew more and more confident that she had made the right decision. Her week flew by, and although she wished she could stay longer, she was excited about heading back to the London office and getting stuck in.

She arrived back to London on Saturday and after a good night's sleep, she headed over to see Mr Adler and to collect Marley.

'Annabel, it's lovely to see you. Come on in.'

'It's good to see you too, Mr Adler. How has it been with him?'

'We had a great time. He was no trouble at all. But you tell me about your travels. How was Paris? Beautiful, isn't it?'

'It was great. Met some lovely people. It's such a great city. Here,' said Annabel, handing him a small packet. 'I've brought you back a little something.'

'How thoughtful of you, but you didn't have to.'

'Don't worry. It's nothing fancy. Just some chocolates.'

They sat chatting for a while and finally, Annabel asked, 'Have you seen James lately?'

'Yes. He came over a couple of days ago. I think it was on Wednesday. He said he'd been away for a few weeks, and he was going away again for a while. I think he said it was for work. Busy chap.'

He's all right then, thought Annabel. 'I tried to call him a few weeks ago, but his phone seemed to be off.'

'Oh, yes, he gave me his new number. Something happened to his old one and he had to change it. He told me about it all, but I can't remember the ins and outs.'

That makes sense now. Why didn't I think of that?

'Let me have a look for you. I'm sure he won't mind me giving it to you. He did ask about you.'

'Did he?' said Annabel, trying to hide her excitement.

'Yes, told him about your new job and that you were away in Paris. I hope you don't mind.'

'Not at all.'

'He seemed very pleased for you. There. I've found it,' he said, passing a piece of paper to Annabel.

A little while later, she headed back to her flat with Marley and contemplated whether to call James. She had waited for over a month, so a couple of more weeks wouldn't make a difference. The idea of speaking to him in person certainly appealed to her more than over the phone. *I'll just wait for him to return, and I'll speak to him then. That'll be the best.*

With her thoughts about James settled, Annabel could focus her attention on other things. She had been enjoying getting stuck into her new role, but she was determined not to make the same mistakes again. She took time to meet up with friends and family, catching up with Lucy and Liv after work, telling them all about her trip to Paris and planning a day out in the city with her mother. She had regular chats with Abi, talking about life in general and the progress on the wedding preparations. She also offered to organise Abi's hen do. Her sister was overjoyed, but conscious that her sister had a lot going on, she suggested that Annabel could organise it together with Ang, her maid of honour. Her friendship with Becca was getting back on track, too.

The book club was coming up in a few weeks and she was getting into the new novel. She looked forward to going again, especially after she heard that Alex had taken a job in America and was leaving very soon.

After a few weeks off, she started to get back into running as well and she was pleased with every little improvement she'd made. Her life couldn't have been going better, but with February over, James still hadn't returned.

***

When March came around, the days started to brighten, and she was glad to wave goodbye to the cold, dark evenings. With increased motivation to carry on running, she was getting better and better each day. Her latest record was five miles in one go, which made her incredibly proud and encouraged her to keep up the hard work.

She woke up early one morning and decided to go for another run in the local park. She turned the corner where she'd run into James a couple of months earlier, almost hoping she'd collide with him again, but today no one was around. Finishing her run, she made sure to complete her stretches before heading home. *Just under five miles. That's not bad.*

She walked up the road and waited at the lights when her eyes stopped on a spot in the distance. A figure was across the street, close enough for her to know it was James. He was with a woman, leading her into a coffee shop, his hand on her back.

The light turned green, but Annabel didn't move, her feet pinned to the pavement. A brief thought crossed her mind. Maybe she could go to the coffee shop after them. *Maybe I could casually run into them*, she thought, before dismissing the idea. She wasn't going to make a scene. She had no right to. *It's not like there was ever anything between us.* She'd hoped there would be, but maybe it was too late, and she'd missed her chance. It wasn't easy, but with her workday starting in just over an hour she pulled her thoughts away from James and jogged back to her flat.

For the remainder of the day, Annabel couldn't help but wonder who the woman was and how long James had been back. *Why didn't he call? He could have at least knocked on my door.*

Now she knew he was back, she could go and see him, but she wasn't sure she was ready for that. Before, she had it all figured out, the way she'd tell him how she felt. But now she couldn't find the words. She could just make small talk and ask about his trip like a good neighbour would, of course, but she wasn't good at pretending. Her eyes would give her away. Despite knowing that addressing her issues head on was the best way, she wasn't ready for that just yet.

So, her plan for the next couple of weeks was avoidance. She hoped she wouldn't run into him before her trip to Verona, and maybe by the time she returned she'd have her feelings figured out, ready to face him. *I can't hide from him forever, but I need more time to figure this out.*

During the next couple of weeks, she left early and came home late and, with the exception of one close call, she had no problem avoiding James.

She arrived at the office early on Friday to finish off any outstanding tasks before her holiday. She'd left her desk tidy the night before, so it was easy to see a manuscript lying there.

This might be my first solo assignment, she thought with excitement. She eagerly picked it up and read the note before peeling it off. After a quick scan through, she headed straight to Iona's office and burst in.

'This manuscript is brilliant.'

'That was fast. Have you read it already?'

'I have. Not today, of course. It was sent to us last year at Herold & Hains. I thought it'd be great to publish, but they had a different take on it. I knew the writer decided to go elsewhere but I wasn't sure what happened to it after that.'

'It's such a compelling story. Here,' said Iona, handing her the author's details.

'Janie made contact with him a month or two ago, but he was out of the country. He's back now. You can reach out to him after your break. He's expecting our call,' said Iona.

Annabel looked at the address and the name.

'Wait a minute. This can't be.'

'What's the matter?'

'This address. The name. He's my neighbour.'

'Really? Well, that's interesting. Has he mentioned it to you before?'

'Never.'

***

On the twenty-third of March, the day finally arrived. After months of anticipation, Annabel couldn't wait to start her holiday. It was only a matter of hours before she boarded the Orient Express to Italy and set off on her adventure. She had made plans to discover the city on a walking tour as well as joining a group daytrip to the countryside.

Lucy took Marley the day before to stay with them for the next couple of weeks and she had everything else sorted. She selected her attire for the journey and was excited that she could finally put on the broad-brimmed hat she had kept in her wardrobe for so long.

Her shock revelation on Friday about James had thrown her somewhat. She had so many unanswered questions zigzagging in her mind, and it made her attempts to get him out of her head all the more difficult. It seemed a big ask, but she made a pact with herself that she'd banish him from her thoughts for the next few weeks and try to enjoy her trip. On the way to Victoria station, she watched the houses rush by the track. It was early in the morning with not many passengers in the carriage. She stifled a yawn as her stop approached.

The train wasn't difficult to spot as she walked into the station. The elegant royal blue carriages were adorned with gold writing and the emblematic Orient Express logo. After locating the platform, she still had plenty of time before her train was to leave, so she headed to a coffee shop to get her morning fix.

With a cup of steaming coffee in her hand, she couldn't resist checking out the bookshelves of the newsagent next door. She had brought a couple of books along for the journey, but there was always room for one more and she was quick to pass her bibliophile obsession off as a necessary hazard of the job.

She flicked through the pages of a few books, but she didn't find anything of particular interest.

When she stepped back from the shelves, she narrowly missed colliding with a woman passing behind her. She apologised and as she turned her head. She stood for a moment motionless, her feet rooted to the ground in shock. Her face was like she'd seen a ghost. *So much for trying to get him out of my head.* Her eyes tried to follow a figure in the distance, but the next time she looked around, they were gone. Content that her eyes must have played a trick on her, she headed to the train.

A helpful steward was quick to assist with her luggage and led her to the compartment. The cabin was beautiful, exactly as she had imagined it to be. The dark wood walls had a glossy finish, and ornate upholstery covered some of the furniture. It was as if she had stepped back in time. With still half an hour left before departure and her bags safely stowed, she was excited to explore the rest of the train, so she headed to the dining car. Walking along the wood-panelled corridors, she felt glamorous in her long sweeping dress. She scanned the room as she reached the dining car and headed to one of the high stools by the bar. She looked through the drinks menu, and not being a big drinker at the best of times, she wasn't sure if starting so early would be a good idea. After some contemplation, she settled on her choice.

'I'll have a L'Oriental, please. A non-alcoholic one,' she said to the man behind the bar.

'Great choice, ma'am.'

'Is there a breakfast service on this morning?'

'There is ma'am. Let me get you the menu,' he said, before tending to her drink.

In between scanning the menu, she watched him mix the ingredients and shake the contents before pouring the concoction into a tall glass. Even without the alcohol, she felt decadent lifting it to her lips.

'Delicious,' she said.

'I'm glad you like it, ma'am. Are you ready to order?'

'Yes, I'll have eggs benedict, please.'

'Could you make that two, please,' came a man's voice from Annabel's right.

She hadn't noticed him when she sat down, hidden behind the morning papers. She turned to face him as he lowered his hands.

'James. What are you doing here?' she asked, a mixture of surprise and slight annoyance in her voice.

'I'm waiting for the train to depart to Verona.'

'Really? What a coincidence. I mean, I haven't seen you in months and of all places we meet here,' said Annabel.

'Well...' James hesitated. 'It's not exactly a coincidence, if I want to be totally honest. I kind of knew you were going to be travelling on here.'

'I don't understand.' Annabel looked puzzled.

'When we took that taxi back from the hospital, I wanted to say something, but it didn't seem the right time. You weren't in the right headspace, and I didn't know how you'd react. When I knocked on your door later, David was there, and I thought... I thought you were back together,' continued James.

'That's why you didn't pick up when I called?'

'I just needed to get my head straight. I thought I'd call you back after Christmas.'

'But you didn't even send me a message.'

'I was going to, but when I finally got to Scotland I couldn't find my phone. I've searched everywhere but I must have left it on the train. It's a long story, but I ended up having to get a new one.'

'But you know that we weren't back together, right?'

'I realised that after a while. It took me a few days to get a new phone sorted with everything closed over Christmas. And when I returned you were still away and I had a trip planned, so I missed you again.'

'I still don't understand. How did you know I'd be travelling on here?'

'Mr Adler. I went to see him when I got back. I think you were in Paris at the time. He told me about your plans and cleared up the stuff about David. Congratulations on the new job, by the way.'

'Thanks. So why didn't you come and speak to me then?' she asked.

'Things were busy with work, and I had to take another trip shortly after that.'

'But you've been back since,' Annabel blurted out. 'I saw you across the street from the park a couple of weeks ago. You were with someone.'

'Did you? You could have come over to say hi.'

'I didn't think you'd be interested. And I didn't want to intrude on your date.'

'My date?'

'With the blond woman. How many dates have you been on?'

'None. You must be thinking of Izabella. I think you've got the wrong end of the stick. She's my new agent. I decided to part ways with my old one before Christmas and I was having a chat with her to see if we could work together.'

'Oh.' Annabel felt foolish; she jumped to the worst conclusion and not considered anything else. But at the mention of the word agent, a flood of questions came to her mind.

'Agent? It's interesting you say that because I had a manuscript left on my desk this week to make contact with the author once I'm back. Do you care to explain about that, Mr M.J. Shaw?'

James hesitated.

'Why did you never mention to me that you write? You knew what I did,' asked Annabel.

'There was nothing to mention, really. It was a debut novel, and my agent handled all the correspondence with publishers. That was one of the reasons why we decided to part ways in the end. She wasn't getting anywhere. Then I'd realised that she'd sent it to Herold & Hains and that you've seen it. When you told me that they wanted me to rewrite the story completely I spoke to her. She was all for it. I just thought it would have changed the essence of the book completely. That's when we parted ways. I knew you had a lot on and I didn't want to drop another surprise on you.'

Things started to make a bit more sense now, and the intensity of Annabel's questioning eased off.

'Hang on a second,' she said. 'You are Avery Poole! Oh my God. That's why you've been so secretive. Is that the dream that you've given up on?'

'Not quite,' said James. 'But I did work for the British secret service. But that's a story for another day.'

Annabel was trying to comprehend the revelations. 'You still haven't told me why you're here. You said you wanted to ask me something,' she said finally.

'I did. I do.' James hesitated, and for the first time, Annabel sensed his nerves. He moved closer to her, taking her hands in his. 'I wondered if I could ask you out on a date.'

Annabel could feel her pulse quicken as she paused for a moment, thinking about the last challenge in the Advent calendar. She smiled.

'It's funny you ask that, because I wanted to ask you the same thing.'

'I take that as yes, then,' he said, as he leant in to kiss her.

When their breakfast arrived, they took their seat at one of the tables.

'It was a bit of a risky move, you coming here. What would you have done if I'd said no?' she asked.

'I don't know. It would have been a bit of an awkward trip I suppose.' James laughed.

As they settled in their seat, the train started to move slowly, leaving the station. Annabel had one last thing to do. She typed out a message a hit send.

The list is complete! See you in three weeks x

I hope you've enjoyed this book and if you have, I'd love if you could leave a review so that others can find it and enjoy it too.

SCAN ME

Acknowledgements

Thank you to Rosie for your invaluable insights, for your thorough and skilled edits that helped me develop this story from its initial stages. Without you this story may have never taken its current form. Thank you to Lena for your beautiful artwork and for helping to bring to life the world I've imagined. Thank you to Laura and Noémi for reading my earlier drafts and for your kind words. Thank you to my writing tutor and fellow writers for your honest feedback on the first draft and for the space that provided me with a structure where I could continue to weave the story each week. And thank you to Robert, for your patience, unwavering support and encouragement.

Printed in Great Britain
by Amazon

33715751R00158